Off Track

By
C.L. Hadyn

Copyright © 2017 by C.L. Hadyn
ISBN: 978-1-68361-176-9
Cover art by Fiona Jayde

Published by
Decadent Publishing Company, LLC

Look for us online at:
www.decadentpublishing.com

~A Note from the Author~

I am so happy to be able to introduce you to Orion Brown and Dai Waleska.

Like many veterans, Orion was seriously affected by the combat he took part in, and the standard methods of treating his PTSD are not working for him. In desperation, Orion will seek an unorthodox solution by submitting to the Dominance of Dai Weleska, a Japanese-American Kung Fu Master, and as reluctant to have a male to dominate as Orion is to submit. Will this unlikely pairing work? Open the pages and see.

C.L. Hadyn

Chapter One

An innocent hug, a brief touch of a soft, feminine body to his hard chest and Orion closed his eyes, wishing he could hold the woman to him for just one second more as she protested his early departure. But he looked over her shoulder, and the scene in the backyard barbecue disturbed him. The grass had faded to a sickly green, and the voices calling encouragement to the men playing horseshoes sounded muted and distorted. Orion stiffened, pasted a polite grin on his face, and murmured his good-bye to the hostess.

The acrid aroma of unclaimed hot dogs turning to charcoal on the backyard grill followed him as he put one foot in front of the other to get to his truck, and, once inside the cab, he ignored the impulse to push the gas pedal to the floor. Peeling out would call attention to his hasty departure. He didn't need an audience. They might ask him questions he couldn't answer.

The Great Spirit must've been smiling down upon him, for he spotted the dirt road in time to take it and park before the isolated road in Jacksonville, North Carolina, disappeared and the brown, dusty hills of Afghanistan took its place. Gunnery Sergeant Orion Brown turned off the ignition and opened a window to dissipate the odor of AVGAS. It made the *whop, whop, whop* of slowing chopper blades all the louder, and he clenched and unclenched his fists to stop them from shaking like a junkie's going through detox.

The smell of burnt oil wrinkled his nose. The cordite on the lance corporal's cammies filled his nostrils while the guy sobbed and clung to him, not giving a fuck about maintaining a macho posture. Orion glanced over the corporal's shoulder and caught the corpsman closing the eyes of the Marine he'd been working on. He'd participated in this maneuver enough times to know what came next. He touched the sleeve of his uniform, and his fingers came away wet with the corporal's tears. Another Marine killed in combat, and his shoulder used for solace.

His gut twisted at the necessity of bucking up another man to face battle without his battle buddy covering his six, and his mouth puckered at the unexpectedly bitter taste of the words he murmured in consolation, but this time his soothing words fell on deaf ears. The Marine who'd sought a measure of comfort for his grief couldn't hear him. The cessation of sobs, and the stillness of the lance corporal's body, sent a zing of fear through him, and he patted the man's cheek. No response. The lance corporal hadn't stopped crying, he'd stopped breathing.

"Corpsman! Goddamn it, help me. This Marine's wounded as well."

His fear made his voice loud and shrill, and everyone in the chopper, who'd been so busy tending the obviously wounded Marine, froze in place. Orion forgave them the startled looks, for no one, himself included, realized the Marine who'd carried his friend to safety had also been wounded and bled out while he cried. Orion ducked his head into the lance corporal's shoulder, and, just this once, sought his own comfort as he rocked the fallen Marine.

He let the corpsman take the body from his arms, but the relief of the weight, strangely, brought unexpected pain. Orion rubbed the center of his chest and had the surreal thought that this was what it felt like when your heart hit rock bottom. He never held anything back, be it giving comfort, or support or advice, so he shouldn't be surprised to find his emotional reservoir empty. Gunnery Sergeant Orion Brown had nothing left to give, and his heart had just free-fallen to hit the rock bottom of an empty well. It made the same damn questions echo all the louder in his mind.

What the fuck am I doing wrong? How can I keep my men safe? I've taught them everything I know. What else is there?

The hard plastic of the steering wheel cutting into his forehead as he slumped against it, and a yell from someone in a passing car to find an actual parking lot if he wanted to sleep in his truck, brought Orion back to North Carolina.

He checked his rearview mirror before putting the truck in gear, and caught his reflection. Yep, same poker-faced expression. He wore it pretty much 24/7 now. He'd developed it especially for visiting the psychologist because, while he might be crazy, no one ever had a reason to call him stupid. If he even hinted at his nightly thoughts of terminating himself, he'd either be a guest in a VA psych ward or a drugged-up zombie. Nope, not happening...at least not today.

Chapter Two

Five days after the barbecue, Orion threw the out-of-date magazine on top of equally old and dog-eared ones on the table in front of him. He turned his gaze to the other patients filling the chairs in the VA waiting room. He preferred to people watch, anyway. Like him, they waited for their names to be called so they could see whichever doctor they'd been assigned to. Aside from complaining of the slowness of getting an appointment, no one really talked about their reasons for being here, and that was just fine with him.

He'd been coming to the VA hospital in Fayetteville, North Carolina once a month since retiring for medical reasons. Long enough now to recognize the reaction as a newbie told casual listeners he had an appointment with one of the shrinks. Not that he could really fault his fellow waiters for their reaction of drawing back and looking for signs of crazy in the eyes, or the telltale bulge of a gun. The nightly news had done a thorough job of covering the incidents where a veteran lost it and shot up the waiting room, until a cop made it unnecessary for the shooter to need a follow-up visit.

Fortunately, he didn't have time to speculate whether he'd ever attain such notoriety. He heard his name called and followed the male nurse back to have his vitals checked before being admitted to Doctor Androla's office.

"How you doin', Gunny?"

Orion liked Doc Androla. He always sounded like a wise guy, despite the medical degree from Johns Hopkins pasted on the wall behind his desk. Guess you could take the boy out of New Jersey, but not out of his voice.

The doc struck him as a pretty laid-back, shrink. He always had a slight grin on his face, and he didn't ever lose his cool. Orion knew from firsthand experience. He'd been pretty uptight at the beginning of these sessions, and now, six months later, he had a better handle on his temper. His fear, not so much, but he'd improved on disguising it.

Orion parked his ass in the recliner across from the doc's desk before answering. "I'm doing okay, Doc."

"Hmm, I might believe that if your blood pressure didn't say otherwise. Were you so eager to see me you rushed to get here?"

Orion snorted in self-derision. "No offense, Doc, but I'd be lying if I said I ever rushed to get here. Coming to the VA hospital is right up there with having a root canal without Novocain."

"No offense taken, Gunny." Doctor Androla swiveled his executive desk chair around to face his patient and crossed his legs.

"You know, Orion, I didn't always want to

become a psychologist. I played around with becoming a police detective, but my mother thought it would be a waste of a good brain if I ended up getting shot by some Mafia wannabe who wanted to make his bones in Nutley, New Jersey. My mother suggested psychology, and in my family no one ever argued with her suggestions.

"To make a long story short, I still haven't lost my detective skills, and they're telling me you had another flashback. Your blood pressure is elevated, your hands are clenched, and you have dark circles under your eyes from lack of sleep. Why don't you tell me what happened?"

"Guess your detective skills are still sharp, Doc. Yeah, I attended a backyard barbecue last week. One of my classes finished a difficult field test and wanted to celebrate. I didn't think there would be any harm in going."

Orion leaned forward in the chair until his arms rested on his knees. "Wow, big mistake. I got out of there before I lost it. At least no one saw me turn into a nut job."

As he knew he would, the doc chastised him for his choice of words.

"You are far from a nut job, a psycho, a fruit loop, or whatever other derogatory words you guys are using these days."

Doc Androla stretched out his legs and crossed them at the ankle before asking, "Do you have any idea what triggered the flashback?"

Orion knew exactly what triggered it, but he didn't want to say so. If he admitted he broke down from a woman hugging him, the doc might try to prescribe one of those little blue pills. He didn't need a four-hour erection accompanying his panic attacks.

"Haven't a clue, Doc. One minute I'm fine, and the next I'm beating feet to keep from showing everyone what a genuine flashback looks like."

He wouldn't win any prizes for best liar, and the look Doc Androla gave him proved it, but, mercifully, he didn't call him on it.

"On your last visit, we went into more depth on survivor's guilt. Has any of that resonated with you? You mentioned...."

Orion pasted a polite look on his face, and nodded where appropriate, but he let the doc's words fade to white noise because he didn't buy the diagnosis. It pissed him off every time the doc said "survivor's guilt." So much so, he fantasized about fieldstripping the civilian like a cigarette butt to discourage him from using those two words ever again.

Orion bit his lip to keep his anger behind his teeth. Deep down, he knew survivor's guilt didn't cause his insomnia, panic attacks, and ever-present depression. The doc just didn't get it. He didn't feel guilt or anything else. Flash frozen would be a better description of what ailed him. No conductivity, no spark, nothing at all. People touched him in the course of training, he even returned their touch, but they left no registrable sensation, not a fucking thing. The few times he'd made a human-to-human connection, like at the barbecue, it resulted in a panic attack that drowned him in a tidal wave of sensation. Bad sensation. Frequent practice made him a champion surfer at riding the panic wave, but the aftermath of numb isolation made him want to put the barrel of his Glock in his mouth and pull the trigger.

Realizing the doc had stopped talking, Orion pasted a sincere look on his face as he hurried into conversation to cover his inattention.

"Hey, Doc, I almost forgot to tell you. That deep breathing thing you taught me really works. It calmed me enough to drive myself home after the attack."

The doc's glance at the clock told him the session had run its allotted time. Orion tried to meet Doc Androla's eyes, but couldn't quite pull it off.

"I haven't given up on you, Gunny, and I hope you don't give up on yourself. My inner detective is telling me you won't be back for another appointment, but I promise you, if you change your mind and decide to give counseling another chance, I'll fit you in, no matter how heavy my schedule."

The doc stood and patted him on the shoulder, and Orion steeled himself before he flinched at the contact. He liked Doc Androla, but he'd struck out with him. Orion quietly closed the door behind himself and suddenly realized, if he wanted to return to a semblance of normal, he'd have to find the cure himself.

Orion sighed in relief as he pulled into his driveway in Sneads Ferry, North Carolina. He'd done nothing for the two hours it took to return from the VA hospital but sink deeper into the blues for not being a cooperative patient.

He shut down the engine, and the somber thoughts, and climbed the steps to the house he'd built overlooking the New River. He'd chosen the location so he could watch the shrimp boats trawl up and down in pursuit of their crustacean harvest. It gave him a measure of peace. Since the river flooded during the occasional hurricane, Orion built his house on stilts with hurricane construction specs.

One of the things he heard Doc Androla mention this morning disturbed him. His choice of the isolated setting for his house pointed toward a desire to cut himself off from interacting with people.

Orion's lips twisted wryly. *Can you say recluse?* With the unexpected appearance of his panic attacks, he'd limited his contact with other Marines outside the classes he taught. People didn't get too many chances to get overly affectionate with Gunnery Sergeant Orion Brown, and it bothered him that his self-imposed exile suited him just fine.

The barbecue last week only reinforced his conviction that parties with wives and girlfriends present occasioned hugging and/or kissing cheeks, which led to panic attacks. He wanted to kick himself in the ass for forgetting that.

Orion hung his keys on the assigned peg, fished a beer out of the fridge, and walked out to the deck to continue his train of thought. Yeah, being around people led to unwanted touching, which almost always led to a panic attack—a very large problem for his civilian career as an instructor for MARSOC or Marine Special Operations Command.

He taught special operations Marines how to track and counter-track, and he excelled at it. He could, no bragging at all, follow a caterpillar's trail through tall grass, but his talent wouldn't be worth a hill of beans if the panic attacks stopped him from teaching.

Orion took a moment to appreciate the sunset and suddenly realized he didn't have many answers to the questions plaguing his waking and sleeping hours, but he did know one thing. He needed to teach because, deep down in his gut, he recognized it as a form of expiation for fucking up in Afghanistan. Imparting his knowledge to Marines to keep them safe gave him a reason to get dressed each morning.

And morning invariably followed night. He knew it did because sleep never came. He'd gotten into the habit of surfing the Web as a productive means to occupy his brain. He actually learned a thing or two about art, history, and do-it-yourself projects during his surfing sessions.

With no ball games or any other shows holding his interest on television this evening, Orion returned to Web surfing but almost gave it up as a lost cause. His fingers kept pushing the wrong keys, demonstrating the relationship between sleep deprivation and manual dexterity. He clicked on a whacko site before his brain could command his finger to cease and desist.

Orion reared back as a suggestive Website popped up. The woman featured in a bustier and stiletto heels, and not much else, got his attention immediately, as did the bold words running across the screen.

Are you a Dominant or a submissive? Do you crave heightened sensation in your relationships? Want to know the answer? Click here.

Once again, without conscious volition, his trigger finger clicked on the *Learn More about Yourself* icon. Orion read the entire ad, but the last line had him switching off his computer with a decisive shake of his head. The BDSM club posting the ad wanted him to fill out an online questionnaire.

Not willing to bare his soul on the Internet,

Orion abandoned the computer and went to bed to peruse the stars through the skylight in his ceiling. He had six more hours of resisting the nightly urge to make a bullet his midnight snack before he could dress and go to work.

Approximately 15:00 Monday afternoon, Orion changed his mind about filling out the online form, as he silently shadowed two of his students who searched for signs to give them a clue which direction he'd taken. They hadn't yet discovered he'd circled around and changed their positions from hunters to hunted.

He approved of the way they watched how they placed their feet, but he frowned at the noise they made. Their whispered conversation carried quite clearly in the stillness of the woods, and he flattened himself underneath a chokeberry bush when they stopped walking.

"Hey, Jason, did you see how fast Gunny Brown took off from the party last Saturday?"

"Yeah, bro. The man probably couldn't chill out even if he parked his ass on a block of ice."

While Orion hardly thought the observation funny, his students obviously did. He started to make his presence known, but they continued.

"Man, I wonder if Gunny is getting any. The dude needs to drain some of the uber testosterone he carries around."

"I agree. But if he hasn't found a woman, he probably has the most calloused palm in the Corps. A guy I know from the class before ours says he's part Lakota Sioux, so maybe he's trying to project a taciturn Native American image, or whatever, but the man looks like he eats nails for breakfast."

"Yeah, I heard a couple of the wives say they gave up trying to talk to him because he answered any question in two words or less. Hell, he barely spoke to us except about tracking. Gunny needs to spend less time communing with trees and brush up on his social skills."

Orion didn't make a habit of eavesdropping on his students, but this one time had been enlightening. His social withdrawal had progressed further than he'd realized, and the thought he might one day forget how to be around people at all made his stomach cramp. When one of the Marines bent down and pointed to a patch of flattened grass, he backed away as silently as he'd tracked them.

"Oh fuck, he's changed directions again. C'mon, we need to stop shooting the shit and concentrate."

Classes over for the day, Orion returned home and shucked his fatigue pants and instructor T-shirt to shower and pull on a pair of worn cargo shorts. He omitted his usual pre-dinner beer in favor of filling out the detailed form to determine if he measured up for Dom or sub. He found some of the questions difficult to answer because what he knew about the BDSM lifestyle could be engraved on a grain of sand. Thanks to his late-night surfing, he'd ascertained interaction between the Dominant and submissive could include pain, but only if consensual. However, the part where yielding personal power to the Dominatrix led to heightened sexual enjoyment for the sub or both parties confused him. How could caving to another person's demands bring sexual satisfaction?

Orion's finger hovered over the mouse as he considered how much of himself he'd have to subsume to submit to anyone. Obeying a military command from a superior officer constituted submission for him. Submitting to a civilian's demands smacked of weakness, until the image of being spanked as a prelude to a spectacular orgasm pinged some deeply buried eroticism.

His students had it right—his chapped palm did show signs of too-frequent use, but a sexy Dominatrix tickling him with a whip might not be a totally repugnant way to draw him out of his frozen shell. At the very least, if it didn't work, he'd be able to check the BDSM scene off the list of things he'd tried in lieu of heavy-duty drugs.

Orion struggled to complete the questionnaire, especially the question asking if pain sexually aroused him. What kind of person would be aroused by pain? He almost hit the delete button until he took a deep breath to consider his response. Did the Plains Indians of the nineteenth century achieve a sexual buzz as a side effect of the pain they experienced during a Sun Dance? Perhaps.

Digging deeper inside himself, he admitted there had been a frisson of sexual enjoyment in completing a twenty-five mile ruck march. Even though he ached everywhere, the march had invigorated him because he'd bested himself or other Marines, and getting his ass slapped and man hugs from other Marines as recognition of his achievement had him exuberantly punching the air. He tried to recall what such satisfaction felt like as he filled in the blanks on the questionnaire.

Last question answered, Orion stabbed the send button and shut off his computer. Time to drink a beer on his deck and watch the shrimp boats return to their marinas for the night.

Chapter Three

Moira Cavendish chose a seat at the back of the restaurant. As a powerful Dominatrix, she enjoyed any opportunity to study men, and highly trained, lethal men at the peak of their physical power filled this restaurant, and many others, in Jacksonville, North Carolina during lunchtime. Jacksonville's proximity to Camp Lejeune and Marine Special Operations Command had a lot to do with it.

Moira ordered iced tea and sipped it slowly while she waited for the man she'd invited to share lunch with her. A powerful Dom, her former student could also add kung fu master to his credits. She'd been drawn to the unusual combination of powers, as well as the exotic packaging, but he didn't move the needle on all of her compass points. Surprisingly, a submissive had captured her heart.

Moira's brought Camden Marquess to mind. A big, tall, brash Texan, he pursued a career as a powerful FBI agent. Only Moira knew of his preference for an even stronger woman to control him.

Not for the first time, a twinge of regret bloomed in her chest because Cam lived so far away. As Special Agent in Charge of the FBI's Houston office, Cam could only break away for his annual leave.

Moira's skin tingled, and warmth seeped throughout her body with the remembrance of how she and Cam made every moment of his last leave count. She did things and gave more of herself with Cam than she did with any other sub.

She squelched the sudden intrusion of guilt, but it made Moira wonder if she'd let the professional distance she tried to maintain with her clients weaken when it came to Cam.

A ripple of disturbance in the restaurant ended her reverie. Ah, the man she'd come here to meet had arrived.

Watching her former pupil walk toward her brightened her mood. Moira had a surprise for him, and it pleased her to think it would not only make him happy, but someone else as well. Moira loved giving presents.

***

Kenjiro Waleska, aka Dai, locked his dojo and hopped on his Harley with a keen sense of anticipation. Moira Cavendish's invitation to lunch had him skirting the speed limit to reach the restaurant she'd selected, for one did not keep Moira Cavendish waiting. It didn't take Dai long to spot Moira, but it did take him longer than he liked to reach her table. Many of his martial arts students stopped him with greetings and small talk. Too polite to brush them off, Dai started to apologize profusely for keeping Moira waiting, but she laughed and waved away his apology.

"It's obvious your reputation precedes you, Sensei."

"Ms. Cavendish, there is no need to address me as Sensei. I am no longer your teacher."

"Touché, Dai. I'll stop calling you Sensei if you stop addressing me as Ms."

Moira leaned across the table and patted Dai's arm.

"I am glad you were able to break free to meet me for lunch. It's been a long time since you were the teacher and I the pupil."

Dai studied his former student. Moira, to put it mildly, turned heads wherever she went. Titian-red hair sparking flames whenever she moved, long legs encased in genuine silk hose, and a body shaped specifically for a man's desire got everyone's attention. No one found it hard to believe it when they were told of her profession.

Moira had entered his dojo a year ago with a proposition too outrageous to pass up. She wanted him to teach her how to defend herself if one of her clients got out of bounds. In return, she would teach him how to be a Dom. His protest of ignorance of the entire BDSM scene died quickly. Moira captured his interest with one move. She'd mesmerized him with a soft caress and a no-nonsense command, and for the first time in his life he assumed a submissive posture.

More than a little turned on, and too shocked to continue protesting, Dai acquiesced to her request. He soon learned Moira had an uncanny knack for knowing the exact location of the switch inside a man. Moira excelled at turning off the alpha and letting the sub come out to play.

A questionnaire designed by Moira easily validated his Dominant strengths, but playing the role of a submissive, while Moira demonstrated Dominant techniques, took some effort. He soon tumbled to the fact Moira used her own style of psychology when working with a submissive. She never broke a man or a woman without rebuilding them in a stronger, better way. Moira didn't believe in submission for her personal dominance, she believed in getting her sub to a higher plane of enjoyment and self-awareness. Her punishments only made the rewards sweeter.

"I have a sub for you, Dai."

He sat straighter in his chair to give his words more gravity. "You know I'm not a practicing Dom. I have enough on my plate running my dojo. I'm too busy to devote the time needed for a submissive."

"No worries, then. This man is not a submissive. He's a Dom in his own right, but I think he needs to try being a switch until he works out his emotional issues."

Dai, who'd sampled his iced tea while Moira continued her explanation, made sure he swallowed all of the tea in his mouth before exclaiming, "A man? You want me to dominate a man? Of all people, I would have thought you knew me better."

Moira waved dismissively. "Pish tosh, Dai. I know what an alpha male you are. I meant no disrespect, but this man is unique. He sees absolutely everything down to the smallest detail, and it's become a problem. He's seen too much, and it has frozen him."

Moira gazed into the middle distance as she chose her next words carefully.

"He wants to feel, to participate with the people around him, but the subconscious barrier he's erected to protect himself from further hurt prevents it. The only way his barriers will come down is if someone more dominant than himself gets him out of his comfort zone. He's become quite cozy in his cocoon. Having to submit to a male's dominance will keep him off-kilter."

Dai's head swung back and forth as he railed at Moira's request. "And what of my comfort? What you are asking of me is not in my nature. As my teacher, I would've thought you'd understand what makes me tick."

Moira grinned at Dai then rubbed her thumbs lightly over the pressure points in his wrists. "You will be the Dom. It is up to you how far you want to go, sexually. What I want you to do is eradicate his aversion to being touched by becoming his guide, or even his enforcer, if necessary. The man has panic attacks if anyone shows him the slightest affection. He's self-aware enough to realize this and has sought an unconventional means of correcting it."

Moira released his wrists, and Dai rubbed his earlobe in concentration. He nodded for his lunch companion to tell him more.

"In my opinion," Moira continued, "he's made an excellent self-assessment. He's too strong-willed for what the VA is offering in the way of counseling, but I think you are stronger. The Dai Waleska I know can bypass his traditional inhibitions and get him out of his own head by exploring his curiosity of areas presently unfamiliar to him. You can then move on to a deeper level of control to fulfill his needs, wants, and desires."

Dai licked his lips. "I've never done this with a woman, and definitely not with another man, and, frankly, I'm skeptical this man will even say more than 'Oh hell, no,' before he tries to punch me out, let alone stand and play after I describe a scene to him."

Moira's eyes fairly twinkled as she laughed at Dai's skepticism. "Oh, I'm positive this man hasn't ever experienced the sexual high of ceding total control to another person. It isn't often I get one of my questionnaires filled in with absolute, total honesty, but his stood out as almost heartbreakingly honest. I want to help him, and I've chosen you to be the instrument."

Moira spoke quickly before Dai could voice further objections.

"I am certain you are a powerful enough Dominant to introduce him to the delightfully aphrodisiacal properties of total obedience. You are a kung fu master, you dominate just by walking into a room, and this man will respond to your power. It will be up to you to take him to levels he hasn't as yet experienced. I must add a caution here, Dai. As a strong alpha, this sub will continually test you by trying to top from the bottom."

She gave a tinkling laugh as she leaned forward to give his cheek a gentle caress. "Having taught you myself, I'm confident you'll break him of thinking he can dominate you."

Intrigued despite himself, he asked, "Who is this person?"

"His name is Orion Brown. He's an instructor like you. He teaches special forces Marines how to track hostiles or how to evade being tracked. Orion served as a Marine gunnery sergeant, but he lost too many of his men in combat, and it has almost destroyed him."

Moira sat quietly, waiting for Dai to digest what she'd told him.

"And Orion Brown has agreed to submit to another man?"

She tossed her gleaming red hair over her shoulder at his skepticism, drawing his and every other male in the restaurant's attention. "He will. I haven't actually told him he will have a Dom instead of a Domme, but I have read his responses to the questionnaire I designed, and I can tell he is becoming increasingly desperate to end his isolation. If I present you as the means for doing that, I'm sure he'll agree, after he gets over the initial shock."

"I'd say good luck with trying to convince an alpha male Marine to willingly submit to another male, but if anyone can do it, you can. Let me know if you are able to get him to agree to meet with me."

He attempted to pick up the check, but Moira waved him off.

"Let me, Dai. It's the least I can do for your agreeing to do this. And you needn't think you have to do this totally on your own. You can call me with questions or problems at any time. If I'm not in, leave a message and I will return your call as soon as I can. Now, I'll follow you to your dojo and drop off the equipment."

Dai, who'd come around to help Moira from her chair, stopped and shot her a surprised look. "What equipment?"

"Ah." Her lips curved in a smile promising

nothing but naughty. "I guess I forgot to mention Orion requested all of his training be done in private. He's trained too many Marines in this area and doesn't want to be outed by being seen frequenting my dungeon. I thought you could train him after hours at your dojo. You have the space, and I'm donating the equipment.

"Don't worry. I'm not talking about the large pieces of furniture like a St. Andrew's Cross or a spanking bench. I know you have a heavy bag and a massage table, and they'll do as substitutes. The equipment I'm leaving with you today consists of paddles, cuffs, restraints, nipple clips, plugs, vibrators. You know, the small things to help your sub focus."

Fifteen minutes later, Dai waved good-bye to the force of nature named Moira Cavendish and picked up the two bags of gear he'd need to thaw Orion Brown. He unlocked the closet in the private exercise room reserved for advanced training and slung the bags inside.

As he climbed the stairs to his living quarters, Dai shook his head at Moira's surprising request. He didn't think the equipment in his closet would ever be used because no way in hell would a macho Marine gunnery sergeant agree to sub for a Dom.

Chapter Four

Orion yanked on his tie as he drove toward Wilmington, North Carolina. He swallowed reflexively, but his arid mouth couldn't complete the action. He tugged again at the silk noose around his neck, and wondered if he couldn't swallow because he'd tied his tie too tight. Damn, his nerves twanged right along with the country and western music blasting from his speakers. He'd arrived home after work yesterday to find, no shit, an engraved invitation from the BDSM club. He'd scored an interview with the club owner.

The invitation instructed him to present himself in business attire. Business attire for him meant well-worn combat boots, Marine cammies, and a black T-shirt. He didn't think the fancy invitation had military apparel in mind, so he'd dug out his "dress for success" suit, a starched white shirt, and a half-decent silk necktie.

In a previous life, a woman told him he looked sexy in a suit. He wondered if she still lived in Jacksonville and whether she was now married with a couple of kids. His mood darkened, and his core temperature dropped at the thought of dating again. It wouldn't matter if he lucked out and found a gorgeous, sexy, single woman because that kind of woman didn't want a man who couldn't carry on the banter and affectionate touches dating couples engaged in.

The bleak thought left him as he steered his truck into a private, gated drive and stopped at the intercom to buzz for admittance. He hoped the security camera didn't have a high enough resolution to pick up his surprised expression when a sultry voice addressed him.

"Welcome to Willows, Mr. Brown. Please pull ahead and park in any available space. You will be shown to the interview room by Miss Stephanie."

Orion stepped out of his truck and, rather than approach the front door, immediately chose to stretch his legs and walk partway around the building. He straightened his tie and the lay of his suit as he did so.

He could see where the estate got its name. Towering willow trees lined the rear lawn. He caught the smell of water from the stream the trees shielded, and his anxiety lessened. If he'd been a child, he would have climbed those willows in a heartbeat. No doubt he'd be able to see for miles while perched in the upper branches.

Don't space out and miss your appointment, you dumb shit. Orion shook his head and ascended the travertine steps to the ornate oak door with beveled glass inserts. He aborted his reach for the doorbell when the door opened and a woman greeted him politely.

"Good afternoon, Mr. Brown. My name is Stephanie. Please follow me."

Walking behind Stephanie dissipated his nervousness. His dormant dick actually gave a small twitch to signal its approval of the woman's assets. He silently complimented the understated dress, but her body rocked his world. Not at all familiar with women's hairstyles, he'd have to say she wore her brunette hair in a sleek, sophisticated twist of some sort. But man-oh-man the strand of pearls at her throat and ears gave off sex-on-a-stick vibes. He wanted to forget he came from an advanced civilization and bend her over a desk. Was his guide a Domme or a submissive?

His erotic imagining halted the moment the beautiful woman ushered him into the library. It had a masculine feel to it, with deep-maroon leather chairs placed on either side of a fireplace featuring a black marble mantle. He took the chair indicated and refused the offer of refreshment.

"Ms. Cavendish will be with you shortly, Mr. Brown. If you require anything while you are waiting, please pull the tapestry cord by the fireplace, and someone will help you."

He enjoyed watching Stephanie leave, and the smile he received just before she closed the door behind her told him she'd known her effect on him.

He'd been shown to a chair, but it didn't mean he had to sit in it. Too out of his element to sit still, Orion studied the titles of the books in the floor-to-ceiling bookcases. He bobbled the book he perused as a woman's voice spoke from behind him.

"Are you a reader, Mr. Brown?"

Orion spun to confront whoever had had the

temerity to sneak up on him. He blamed the thick carpet for being taken by surprise.

Orion stared at Moira Cavendish. He couldn't even think, let alone speak. The twinkle in her beautiful eyes told him his openmouthed gawping hadn't offended her. The manners his mother taught him made him force down his nervousness and resume his seat—only after Ms. Cavendish seated herself in the other wing chair.

Moira sensed imminent flight and immediately asked, "Would you join me for a drink, Mr. Brown? Willows has an injunction against drinking alcohol if play is involved, but members who aren't engaging in play are free to imbibe, and I have seen my last client of the day. However, I will forego it if you do not care to join me."

No man—except a recovering alcoholic or a religious teetotaler—would refuse her, even if they didn't care for the taste of whisky. She wanted to put Orion at ease, and having a glass to hold, if not drink from, would take his mind off the nervousness evidenced by a ramrod-straight spine and his position at the edge of his seat. At his slow nod, she pressed the buzzer under the edge of the occasional table next to her chair.

Her questionnaire told her many things about her clients but not what they looked like. She knew Orion would exude an alpha male presence, but she hadn't expected exotic. His eyes, two pieces of obsidian, would have been more at home on a bird of prey than a man. He had jet-black hair without a hint of curl. She'd imagined short hair, even a military cut, and he did wear the sides short, but the longer top fell engagingly over his forehead. She wanted to run her fingers through it. But the color of his skin intrigued her the most. For a man who spent most of his days outdoors she'd expected the dark color. But his taut, cinnamon-colored flesh fascinated her.

Moira stopped her perusal at Stephanie's knock and remained silent as she entered with a tray containing two cut crystal glasses, a decanter of excellent scotch, a bowl of ice, and a small pitcher of water.

"Thank you, Stephanie. I'll do the honors. I hope you like the taste of scotch, Mr. Brown. This one is a favorite of mine because it has a bite but it's not overly peaty. How do you take your drink? Neat, on the rocks, or with a splash of water?"

"On the rocks, please."

As a Dominatrix and an inveterate flirt, Moira would have ensured her fingers touched Orion's when she offered him his drink, but for this client she refrained from tactile contact. She extended the glass on a level palm, and waited as he delicately picked it up without touching her skin. As Orion softened his rigid shoulders and waited for her to take the first sip, she relaxed.

Hmm, the man has manners. A nice fillip to his better-than-average choice of suits and his lean runner's body. She would most certainly, as a prelude to play, have licked behind his ear to see if he tasted like cinnamon or perhaps one of those tiny, sinfully spicy red-hot candies.

She almost asked if he tasted as delightfully scrumptious as he looked, but her training translated her thoughts into a socially acceptable question.

"What is your ethnicity, Mr. Brown? I only ask because I don't believe I've ever encountered such a beautiful shade of skin."

Orion's lips curved shyly upward at her question, and she briefly regretted assigning him to Dai for training.

"I guess, if you want to be blunt, you could call me a half-breed. My father is full-blood Lakota Sioux, and my mother is of Swedish extraction. I got my father's skin and hair coloring, and my mother's tall genes. Native Americans are not generally six feet tall."

"Let me be the first to say, you wear your parents' genes well. Tell me, is Orion a Lakota name?"

"My Lakota name is Sky Hunter. My mother chose Orion, the Hunter or Archer constellation, to correspond. We didn't live on a reservation, and she didn't want me teased by children who had no familiarity with Native American customs."

Moira deemed Sky Hunter Brown to be as relaxed as he ever would be, and got down to business.

"I've studied the questionnaire you filled out, and I don't think I'll surprise you by saying you are a Dominant. What I'm about to say will not please you, but I would ask you to listen to my observations before making a decision. You are under no obligation to follow my counsel, but I believe my plan of action for you can help you function better in society."

He smoothed the side of his thigh before taking a taste of his drink. His brief display of nerves endeared him to her.

She sipped her drink to give him a second to compose himself before continuing. "You strike me as a man who values bluntness where it is needed, which is why I'm going to speak plainly. No one I presently employ here at my club is Dominant enough for you, but one of my former pupils is. If you agree to become a switch for training."

Moira hastened to explain when Orion's eyes narrowed. "A switch is a Dominant who agrees to play a submissive role for a particular purpose or with a particular partner."

Orion's lips compressed to a straight line, but he did appear to be considering her offer.

"I almost didn't complete your questionnaire, Ms. Cavendish."

He broke eye contact and slowly set his drink on its assigned coaster.

"I found your questions exceedingly intrusive at times, and I am not in the habit of laying my soul bare to strangers. The fact I filled out your form should tell you how disappointed and fearful I've become over the failure of more traditional ways to cure my feeling of isolation. You can't see the internal battle I'm carrying on with myself, but it's there. I'm disappointed with your assessment, but I'll try to swallow my Dominant tendencies."

With a huff of resignation rather than eagerness, Orion asked, "Is it possible to meet the woman you've chosen to be my Mistress right now?"

Moira withheld her answer for a long three count. "Before I give you a name, let me give you my assurance the person I've chosen for you has remarkable patience, empathy, and the internal strength to keep you from trying to assume the

Dominant role. I also assure you, whatever the two of you decide is the best contract for easing you into a more comfortable interaction with the people around you will stay between the two of you."

She gave him further assurance with a crisp, "There will be no public displays to cause you embarrassment. All play will be conducted in a private location, as you requested."

After Orion nodded his agreement, she slowly crossed one long leg over the other, and leaned forward to reveal a bit more cleavage. She knew she'd made the right choice for him when the man's gaze did not move from her face. Only a powerful Dom would be strong enough to crack Orion Brown wide open and let him heal with his nerve endings intact.

"Your Dom's name is Ken Waleska," she told him. "He is a martial arts master and, obviously, male."

She waited until he finished spluttering his objections.

"Yes, he was as surprised by my request he serve as your Dom as you are to have him. It took my considerable powers of persuasion to get him to agree to take you as a client."

"But, but...." He flinched and retreated into his seat.

Moira knew exactly the objection Orion wanted to make but couldn't get out.

"Sex can be a part of your training, or not. This is something you and your Dom can work out as you discuss what the boundaries are. However, let me say, if you narrow your choices too much, I doubt even Mr. Waleska can help you.

"You wanted an unconventional approach, and

I'm offering you one. It doesn't have to involve intercourse, but you need to assess your limits, subliminal fears, and desires. Ken will help you do so by whatever means are agreed upon. Meet with him and talk to him. The key to any D/s relationship is frequent and honest communication. Ken is an excellent listener, and I have a good feeling about this."

Orion closed his eyes. "How long do I have to make up my mind?"

She laughed. "Mr. Brown, you can take as long as you want. This is not a hard sell or some sort of bait-and-switch scam. I'm not going to force you to do anything you do not want to do. If I had a woman who could meet your needs, I'd tell you her name right now. If you are unable to accept my referral, give me a call, and I will inform Mr. Waleska. I only ask for an answer within a reasonable amount of time. I don't think it's fair to keep Mr. Waleska waiting."

She touched the buzzer and stood, signaling the interview had ended.

"It has been a pleasure to meet you, Mr. Brown. I sincerely hope you find what you are searching for, whether it be through my referral or by other means."

At Stephanie's appearance, Moira turned to Orion and directed, "Please give Mr. Brown one of my personal business cards. It has my direct number. I'd appreciate knowing your decision as soon as you make it. If you decide to go forward, I will set up a meeting with Mr. Waleska and inform you of the time and place."

She waited until the beautiful man walked silently from the room before crossing her fingers for luck. She fervently believed Orion could be helped if he accepted her choice, but alpha males and strong Doms could often bite off their noses to spite their faces.

Chapter Five

It took him one week to accept Moira Cavendish's proposal. One long fucking week of lying in bed and wondering, if he didn't try this, would he be passing up the only way to rid himself of the panic attacks and regain the ability to interact with people? One week of swearing he wouldn't cede absolute power over himself to any man or woman, and most of all, no man would ever touch any part of his body for any reason, except in the course of training or for an impersonal greeting.

His outraged male reaction caved as he remembered the way the woman offered him the glass of whisky. She'd refrained from touching him because she knew, from his answers on the questionnaire, he had a serious problem with anyone touching him. Had she done it as a courtesy to him, or had she done it to avoid him wigging out in her office? Who the hell knew her reasons, but he had to be honest with himself. He *would've* wigged out if she'd touched him longer than a nanosecond. His painful self-assessment made him screw up his courage enough to hold his place on the sidewalk in front of the Jade Dragon Dojo.

He'd arrived early. Once a Recon Marine, always a Recon Marine. He'd walked around the entire two-story building and discovered a rear entrance which would ensure privacy. From a drugstore across the street, he'd had a clear view of the large plate-glass windows in the front of the dojo, watched the students performing their katas and even a sparring match between two of the pupils.

He couldn't pick out the instructor, Ken Waleska, from the adult class because everyone wore the same white gis. Once the students had left and the dojo windows darkened, he decided the time had come to introduce himself.

It took every ounce of his intestinal fortitude to ring the doorbell. He'd waited for combat to begin with fewer butterflies in his stomach. Mercifully, he didn't need to ring twice. The door opened, and the man who would control his life for however long it took to return him to normal greeted him. Which, now that he saw Ken Waleska up close, might take a long time.

Moira's choice for his Dom surprised him. For one thing, the man couldn't possibly be Polish, as the name Waleska implied. And two, no Asian he knew could put a check mark on the height chart next to six foot two. But he found the Dom's bright jade-green eyes his most startling feature.

The man's lips twitched and Orion snapped out of his rude silence. *Great first impression, Brown. Stare at your Dom like he has two heads.*

Orion's tongue attached itself to the roof of his mouth as he tried to come up with an appropriate greeting. How *did* one greet a Dom? Maybe he should just turn around and get the fuck out of the dojo.

"Welcome, Mr. Brown. Please follow me. My living quarters are on the second floor. I think it will be a more comfortable setting for our discussion. Have you eaten yet?"

Orion croaked a response. "No, I haven't eaten."

He stopped himself from adding, "Unless you count swallowing a shitload of butterflies on the way to this meeting as eating."

"Excellent. I've prepared a simple stir-fry. You may join me, but let me introduce myself first. I am Ken Waleska. Yes, I know my appearance doesn't match my name. I got the Polish name, height, and eye coloring from my father, and my black hair and shape of my eyes from my Japanese mother.

"Most of my friends use my nickname, Dai. It means big in Japanese. Ken is short for Kenjiro. I also answer to Kenji. However, if you accept the contract, you will address me as Sensei. Now, if you don't mind, I will leave you while I grab a shower. There is beer in the refrigerator. Help yourself."

Orion did help himself to a beer. He needed it to wet his throat enough to squelch further croaking. Whatever the sensei had made for dinner smelled quite good, and his stomach voiced with a rumbling growl its willingness to sample it.

The sensei had unconventional living accommodations. Japanese rice-paper screens divided the long upper floor into separate rooms. He'd been shown to the living room/dining area, an area carpet with the texture of velvet and the color of grass covering the bamboo floor. The unusual black-lacquer furniture with its short legs drew his attention. The dining room chairs had no legs at all, merely cushioned seats and backrests.

Apparently, the sensei preferred Japanese living to Western. He also preferred no clutter. The only ornamental pieces consisted of a rosewood katana stand and a single flower arrangement under a hanging scroll. He studied the simple but rather complex appeal of the arrangement, and the word *ikebana* popped into his mind. He'd watched a YouTube video on the art of flower arranging on one of his many late-night surfing bouts.

He stepped away from the arrangement as he heard the sensei call out.

"Could you grab me a beer while I get dinner ready?"

Orion took a slow, relieved breath when he turned around to find Ken completely dressed in jeans and a T-shirt. Noting Kenji's bare feet, he had an "oh shit" moment. He remembered, once again courtesy of the Web, Japanese never wore shoes indoors. His sneakers suddenly stood out like clodhoppers. "I'm sorry. I didn't think about removing my shoes when we came upstairs."

Orion returned quickly to the door and toed his shoes off, placed them neatly on a wooden tray with a pair of flip-flop sandals on it, and went to fetch the sensei's beer.

"Relax, Mr. Brown."

The sensei's calm voice eased the jittering in his gut.

"I think we are both a little nervous this evening."

"Give the man a cigar," Orion muttered before he could discipline himself. On an audible exhale, he asked, "Could you please call me Orion, Sensei? I am more comfortable with my actual name."

"As you wish, Orion. Come, let's both relax and enjoy the meal. After teaching classes all day, my appetite is worthy of a dragon."

Dai waited while Orion seated himself on the legless chair. Most Westerners could not seat themselves without some awkwardness. It pleased him to discover Orion had a natural economy of movement. He made it seem graceful.

He'd already determined to begin Orion's training with a subtle action. If this small test proved successful, it would tell him his decision to use an iron fist in a velvet glove would be the best way to reach the sub. Picking up his chopsticks, Dai selected a slice of pickled ginger and held it up to Orion.

"Here, try this. It's ginger and very good. It's also good for you. Ginger soothes the stomach."

He waited as Orion nervously stared at the offering before him, and he could see the internal debate taking place written large on the man's face. Should he open his mouth or not? If he took the morsel from another man's chopsticks, what signal did it send?

Dai kept his offering rock steady and beamed his approval when Orion leaned forward and took the ginger directly into his mouth. "If you are not familiar with using chopsticks, I can get you a fork."

"Uh, no, Sensei. I can use them. I'm a little clumsy with using them to eat rice, but I can generally get through a meal."

Orion's admission gave Dai another opportunity.

Putting his chopsticks aside, he rose in one movement and placed himself alongside Orion. "Here, let me demonstrate how to hold them to eat your rice."

Dai took the chopsticks from Orion and aligned them correctly before returning them. He did not release his grip as he directed Orion to raise the rice bowl to his lips. Dai only returned to his seat after Orion, with his encouragement, successfully lifted a small, sticky clump of rice to his mouth.

"Excellent, Orion. You are a fast learner."

He did not offer more instruction for the remainder of the meal. He had his small victory. His sub hadn't realized he'd been intimately touched during the course of the demonstration.

Once the table had been cleared and the dishes put into the dishwasher, he directed Orion to the sofa for the post-dinner contract discussion.

Dai opened the negotiations with a bang. "Tell me about yourself, Orion, and what you expect from me?"

He remained silent as the other man mastered his shock at such a direct question.

Orion spoke softly. "Like you, I'm mixed race. My father is Lakota Sioux or Native American. My Lakota name is Sky Hunter, and since we didn't live on a reservation, my parents gave me the corresponding name of Orion in the belief I wouldn't stand out too much." Orion displayed his deep-copper arm and snorted in self-mockery.

"My mother is from Lindsborg, Kansas," he went on. "It is a historical Swedish settlement. As you can see, I have Native American coloring, but I got my height from Mom's side of the family.

"I grew up in Colorado, where my dad is a police officer and my mom an elementary school teacher. My father is a tracker, and has quite a number of rescues to his name of hunters or hikers who aren't local and get lost in the mountains. I learned tracking from my dad.

"I'd gotten halfway through college, but the World Trade Center came down, and I joined the Corps. The Marines quickly recognized my tracking abilities, and I got into Force Recon."

Orion stopped speaking, and Dai tilted his head to encourage him to continue.

"I attended college because both my parents had, but until I joined the Corps I didn't know what I wanted to do for a career. I'd planned on making a career of the military until I lost too many men and got medically discharged because of PTSD. I guess I should be grateful I had good friends who recognized my tracking utility because they convinced me to apply for the job at Marine Special Operations.

"I enjoy working with Marines. At least, I did enjoy it until the panic attacks started to become more frequent." Orion swept his eyes down at the carpet and gave a slow, disbelieving head shake. "You want to know what I want from you? The easy answer would be to help me get rid of my PTSD. But I have serious doubts I can be cured." He scrubbed his face vigorously. "I've never engaged in BDSM before, and never in my wildest dreams did I even consider doing it with a man, but...." He forced the words from his throat as he avoided looking at Ken Waleska. "Okay, I want to be able to be around people again without having to excuse myself for a private meltdown if they offer me any kind of affection or touching. If anyone touches me, even casually, I panic and flash back to losing my men in combat, and having their battle buddies cry on my shoulder. I stayed strong for them, but now I can't relax. I can't let myself...." His voice shook. "I'm afraid I've withdrawn so far into myself I can't ever return, Sensei."

The bald honesty of Orion's admission impressed him, and he asked, "How do you think I should go about getting you to relax or engage with people without causing panic attacks?"

Dai breathed easier when Orion's clenched fists relaxed long enough to wrap them around his knees.

"I've done a little reading on BDSM, and I know there can be spanking or whip work or, um, cuffs involved, but I don't understand what they mean by getting the submissive to subspace." Orion turned in the direction of the flower arrangement and appeared to be studying it. "What I find most disturbing is every Website I've visited talks about sex between the Dom and the submissive." Orion laughed bitterly. "I will be honest with you and say sex might happen if you were a woman, but, no offense, Sensei, it's not going to happen with you. I'm hetero. You will not be sticking your dick in any part of me. Am I being honest enough for you, Sensei?"

Dai forgave his sub his moment of sarcasm. He'd expected such a reaction. However, he would not fill in the blanks for Orion. His sub had to learn how to communicate with his Dom, but he could offer a small prompt.

"If not sex, then what? No, Orion, do not shift away from me. Tell me what you want so I may fulfill it."

Prepared to wait for an answer, Dai grinned up

at his sub as he stretched out and put his head in the man's lap. He gambled Orion would freeze rather than push him away, and he won.

Very aware of how much his action flustered the man, Dai spoke. "I'd say your response sounded like a Dom, not a submissive. Moira told me you've agreed to be a switch, specifically, to forego your Dom inclinations to play a submissive role."

He added a deeper timbre to his voice. "You are not the Dom here, I am. You do not get to decide how the play will progress, I do. You will choose a safe word so I don't inadvertently hurt you."

Reaching up, he ran his thumb over Orion's eyebrow and down the side of his face with the lightest of touches. Though his sub held his arms crossed tightly on his chest, no overt panicking occurred.

"I swear to you, everything I do will be to help you overcome your present problems. If you are in pain or frightened by something I am doing, you will use your safe word, and I will cease what I am doing, immediately, and we will discuss what frightened you, and if you can't or don't want to continue the play, we won't. However, if you use it every time you get the least bit outside of your comfort zone, you might as well return to the VA and start swallowing those tranquilizers they've prescribed for you.

"The whole purpose of BDSM is to take yourself outside of yourself by willingly giving consent over to another person, namely, me. And from what you've told me, you do need to get outside the self you presently are."

Dai sat up suddenly, and Orion flinched. "You should also know a good D/s relationship involves mutual gratification. Curing you of your fear of being touched is only half the job. You should be able to touch others without having to steel yourself to do it. I would hope, with time and effort, you will be able to give as well as receive. Namely, you will learn to touch me with as much feeling as I touch you."

"A D/s relationship is not a vanilla exercise where everyone plays by socially acceptable rules. I will command and control you, and you will obey, unless it is something you feel you cannot tolerate. But if you want vanilla, tell me now, so I can say it's been a pleasure meeting you and sharing dinner, and let me show you the way out of my home."

Dai returned to his supine position on Orion's lap, and snuggled in deeper before closing his eyes to wait for his answer. Being so physically close, Dai's head rose and lowered with Orion's sighed capitulation.

"I'll do it."

"Yes, Sensei, I'll do it," Dai corrected.

"Yes, Sensei, I'll do it," Orion parroted.

Dai sat up immediately, and removed a chain with a dog tag attached from beneath his T-shirt. The tag had a black, rubber ring around it like the ones the Marines used to keep their dog tags from making noise. He held it out to Orion.

"Ours will not be a Master/slave contract, so you don't have to display this," he explained.

"I am giving you this depiction of a dragon to wear to help you focus on who is the Dom. I am the Jade Dragon, and you are my sub. Even though you don't have to keep it visible, you will never take it off unless I direct you to do so. You will assume this submissive posture when you first greet me."

Dai knelt down and sat on his haunches, palms up, and his head bent in demonstration.

He then rose and faced his sub. "May I know your safe word now?"

After a few moments, Orion blurted the word "sponge" into the pregnant silence.

Dai schooled his facial muscles into immobility at the unusual choice but gave no comment other than to order, "Come, let me show you the playroom downstairs."

Dai waited as Orion inspected the room with its wall-to-wall floor mats, a large hanging bag dedicated to practicing punches and kicks, and the padded massage table for easing knotted muscles. He could almost see the nervousness emanating from his submissive, but the moment had come to push him into a firm commitment. The verbal one he'd given upstairs had been too easy.

After what he planned to do, Orion would either have the courage to move forward or disavow all knowledge of having met him, and he wouldn't have wasted a lot of his time training someone who didn't have the courage to see it through.

Grabbing the pair of cuffs he'd deliberately left lying on the massage table after his last class, Dai faced Orion and barked, "Strip."

"Wha...what? Why?"

Dai used a pressure point on Orion to send him to his knees. "Incorrect response. The only response you can make is 'Yes, Sensei.' I will repeat myself this one time. Strip."

Orion's "Yes, Sensei," came reluctantly, but he did undress. Dai would have to work on verbal responses. He would not let the man get away with trying to top from the bottom.

Orion's sidelong glances spoke volumes about his comfort level with standing in front of him without his clothes, but his own sub experience told Dai Orion would soon become inured to being nude in this room. Right now, Orion Brown had things other than nakedness to consider.

Dai gestured to the hanging bag and ordered, "Stand with your back to the bag and grasp the chain at the top."

He halted Orion as soon as he started to comply. "I didn't hear a 'Yes, Sensei.'"

"Yes, Sensei."

After Orion complied and stood with his torso against the leather bag, Dai cuffed him to the chain then addressed his sub, who glanced everywhere in the room but directly at him.

"I know you are wondering what I'm going to do. Relax, Orion. Nothing is going to happen this evening. I merely want to see what I have to work with. You are physically fit. Good muscular definition." Dai ran his palms over Orion's pectorals and down his flat stomach. He stopped right above the pubic hair when a slight tremor registered in his fingertips. "Now, pay attention. You will return here each Saturday night at six o'clock. You won't encounter any of my students because I only teach for half the day on Saturday. You will bring a change of clothes and toiletries in an overnight bag. You will use the key I give you. It's for the rear entrance. You will take a shower in the bathroom off this room, and you will be nude and in the submissive posture waiting for me. For your first and subsequent sessions, you will trim the hair under your arms and your pubic area."

"Shave? Why do I need to shave those places?"

Dai pulled the short hairs above Orion's dick for the temerity he'd shown in questioning his command. Orion's reaction surprised him. The small dose of pain he administered made his student's eyes fall to half-mast, and that small clue made him think his sub might have depths worth plumbing.

He tested his theory by tugging a little harder, until he drew a hiss of pain from Orion. "You haven't given the correct response. Since this is new to you, I'm going to answer your question. You will comply because I, as your Dom, have ordered you to. You as my submissive will please me by saying, 'Yes, Sensei,' and showing up with trimmed armpits and pubis. If you question my directives once training begins, I will punish you. Do you understand?"

He called on his martial arts training to keep his face devoid of reaction until he heard the only thing he wanted to hear from his sub.

"Yes, Sensei."

Dai had learned from Moira that there was a point where pushing a sub became non-productive, so he didn't comment, and released Orion from the cuffs. "You may dress now."

Dai compressed his lips to keep the laugh inside as he watched his sub set speed records shimmying into briefs, jeans, and T-shirt.

"Here is the key. You will be here by six o'clock on Saturday. You will have your dragon necklace on, you will be trimmed, showered, in the submissive posture, and waiting for me at the appointed time. Do you understand?"

Orion didn't face him directly, but the response

he'd been taught in the short time rang loud and clear.

"Yes, Sensei."

Chapter Six

O rion noted his shaking hands as he picked up the bar of soap to begin his shower. For the hundredth time since he unlocked the rear door to the Jade Dragon Dojo, he wondered if he would actually go through with this. The waiting and deliberating on whether or not to attempt this had worn his nerves raw. It had also rubbed him raw to submit to the sensei's order to trim the hair under his arms and above his dick. He'd complied, but not exactly. He'd completely shaved the hair under his arms but left the pubic hair. He hadn't signed up to be a damn stripper.

His wrinkled fingertips told him he'd showered long enough. Once out of the shower, he dried his skin thoroughly. But no matter how vigorously he rubbed the towel over his body, he couldn't eradicate the goose bumps covering him from head to foot. A total body tremor began as he knelt in the playroom and assumed the subservient position. He hoped the sensei would not keep him waiting for too long. Trying to anticipate the unknown was a bitch.

Dai bowed his head before the playroom's closed door and took a calming breath. Once he opened the door, he would be committed to Orion Brown. Truly committed. The whole ball of wax, no shying away from sex play, if Orion needed to go there, and he honestly thought he did. Orion Brown needed to be stripped down to the bone and remade. He needed to be sprung from the confining prison of his own sense of duty and obligation to a place where he could feel good about letting someone else assume the heavy lifting.

With a mental "It's showtime," Dai put his sensei face on and opened the door. Finding Orion in the sub position pleased him. The man did possess steel balls, after all. Dai knew most uber males with Orion's problem would have run to the pharmacy to fill their tranquilizer prescriptions rather than be in this room.

He made sure to caress Orion's cheek as he bent down and commanded, "You may rise."

"Thank you, Sensei."

Dai bit the inside of his cheek to keep his reaction to his sub's appearance from his face. He'd been right. His sub defied him by not carrying out his order to trim his hair. Knowing he'd have to show Orion who had earned the title of Dom, he'd come prepared.

"You will please lean the top half of your body over the massage table."

He'd kept the command vague to gage Orion's reaction. Most men would only bend nude over a table if such an order came from a doctor. Dai gave Orion points for responding "Yes, Sensei," and walking to the table. He wouldn't deduct any points for the fact he did it reluctantly.

To put his sub in a calmer mood, Dai explained, "I thought I'd begin with accustoming you to my touch. I want to introduce you to the feel of my body against yours. Do you remember your safe word?"

"Yes, Sensei. It's sponge. My safe word is sponge."

Dai moved very slowly as he secured Orion to the massage table. There would be no grabbing or harsh pressure for Orion's first serious experience with restraint.

"Sponge it is. I will stop every so often and ask you how you are doing. You can either answer fine, or not good, or you can use colors like green for good, yellow for getting uncomfortable, or red for stop, I've had enough. Or you can simply say sponge and I will stop. Do you understand these directions?"

"Yes, Sensei."

With Orion firmly secured to the table, Dai stepped behind his sub and stroked slowly over his sub's left butt cheek. He stopped and waited when his sub's body began to tremble. He waited for the word sponge to be spoken, but his sub merely turned his head away. Dai swept his palm up the small of Orion's back to the nape of his neck, and down to his right butt cheek. "How do you feel, Orion?"

He grunted, "Green, Sensei."

The tremors shaking Orion's body negated his words. Dai had anticipated his alpha sub wouldn't admit to feeling afraid. And if he wouldn't admit it, then a safe word couldn't be used. His sub had forgotten his warning about trying to top from the bottom.

Dai deliberately stopped and stepped away from the table. The time had come to introduce his sub to a little punishment.

Orion couldn't stop shaking like a leaf. His ego castigated him for his less than he-man, macho Marine-warrior reaction. Until now, he'd thought his combat experience had shown a certain amount of bravery, but having such a spastic reaction to being touched made him question it. He seriously considered saying the safe word as the sensei got a little too close to the crack of his ass, but, fortunately, he hadn't lingered there. Orion had sucked it up and bitten his tongue to keep from embarrassing himself.

"Eyes on me, Orion."

Orion turned his face away and tucked his chin into his neck after noting what Dai held in his hand. It took him several convulsive swallows to get the question out. "Whaa, what are you going to do, Sensei?"

"This is to be part of your punishment for lying to me. You lied about being comfortable, but I know by the tremors racking your body, you aren't. How can I keep from hurting you if you lie to me? This is a relationship built on trust, Orion. I trust you to tell me when you hurt or are uncomfortable with what I'm doing, and you must trust me to stop as soon as you tell me.

"I warned you trying to top from the bottom would bring punishment, and now it has. I ordered you to trim the hair under your arms and pubic region, but you haven't obeyed."

Orion, mesmerized by the basin of hot water and razor, didn't resist as Dai unshackled him and ordered him to climb up on the table. Once his legs had been secured to either side of the table, with his arms extended above his head, he had to force his attention back to understand the sensei's question.

"Are you ready for your punishment?"

Orion wanted to use his safe word and yell, "Sponge, sponge, sponge," but his pride made him say, "Yes, Sensei."

It took everything he had in him to not flinch or fight his restraints as Dai spread the shaving cream around his privates, and, again, he had to concentrate very hard to understand the sensei's next words.

"As your Dom, I cannot tolerate such deliberate defiance. For your disobedience, I am going to shave your pubic area as bald as a newborn's. Do I need to caution you to remain completely still as I shave so close to such a vital organ?"

"N-no, Sensei."

It seemed like an eternity but probably only took a half hour for the sensei to remove all of the hair. His body ached from holding it so still because the sensei made sure he maintained contact with his skin, and the last thing he wanted was to give him any reason for holding him more forcefully. At least he couldn't accuse the sensei of molesting him because he never touched his dick with any sexual intent. He made it seem like a nurse shaving a patient for surgery.

While his mind tried to grasp the subtleties between the sensei's punishment and pleasure, his dick appeared to know the answer. As much as he tried to suppress his reaction to being shaved, it had responded in a most un-hetero way. He'd been so up in his head, the sensei's voice made him jerk the restraints.

"Now is the time for after care, Orion. I've gotten you out of your comfort zone enough for one day, so I'm going to release you."

His response of "Thank you, Sensei," resonated loud and clear, and he noticed it made his Dom grin.

His first session ended with a massage. He floated away from his body as the sensei smoothed the knots and kinks caused by twanging nerves. He must have had a bunch of them because it took considerable time to work them all out. Had he been capable of speech, he would've apologized for the extra time it took.

Orion had had massages before his PTSD made it impossible to even consider having another. But his Sensei had magic in his hands, and even though Dai stroked, kneaded, and caressed him, he didn't object. He could swear his skin hummed a contented tune. It took a light tap on his shoulder to make him shed the cocoon of pleasure he'd wrapped around himself.

Dai tossed him a bottle of water.

"Drink this and drink more after you get home. You'll need to rehydrate for the remainder of this weekend. You may either shower or get dressed. I recommend leaving the oil on until you go to bed."

"I'll get dressed, Sensei."

Right before the sensei opened the outside door to release him for the evening, he stepped up and bumped his chest into his.

"We will part with a hug, Orion."

The sensei's very strong arms enveloped him in a firm hug. His surprise short-stopped the flinch.

"Whenever you feel you are ready, you may return my hug. Good night, Orion. Sleep well."

Not knowing what else to say, he parroted, "Good night, Sensei," and got the hell out of there.

He had to set the cruise control on his truck. He couldn't keep an even speed, and he didn't want to attract the attention of the police, who trolled Route 17 waiting for anyone driving erratically after a Saturday night of drinking. His problem had nothing to do with drinking. He couldn't steer a straight course because he couldn't keep from squirming around in the seat.

His jeans rubbed his shaved groin, and the unaccustomed sensitivity kept making him move to find a more comfortable spot. Lesson learned. If the sensei told him to do something and he didn't comply, he could expect some sort of punishment, and it didn't take too much thinking to know he wouldn't like whatever the sensei dreamed up.

Reaching home without incident, he made a beeline for the shower. He wanted all traces of what he'd done this evening to disappear down the drain. By the time he stepped out of the shower, fatigue hit him like a freight train, and he decided to forego food in favor of crawling into bed.

As his overstimulated brain and body tried to wind down, he got an instant recall of everything he had willingly submitted to in the playroom. His ears grew warm in embarrassment at some of the things he'd let happen without even a weak protest.

God, he hoped this worked because he'd probably die of mortification if it didn't. He'd remove himself from the planet before he'd try anything this drastic again.

Bright light woke him, and he searched his bedroom in confusion. The sun streaming through his skylight told him he'd slept beyond his usual five a. m. rising. Orion turned over in bed and cursed at the time displayed on his digital clock. Eleven o'clock Sunday morning. He'd slept six hours more than he usually did. Actually, he corrected himself, he didn't usually sleep at all. He didn't call the one or two hour catnaps he managed, sleeping.

His stomach didn't care whether he slept or not; it wanted food and gurgled its annoyance at not being given sustenance for such a prolonged period. More than ready to satisfy it, he eased out of bed. He raised his eyebrows when he noticed his bedding appeared not to have been slept in at all. He must have passed out completely as soon as he climbed into bed the previous evening.

As he stretched like a cat beside his bed, he suddenly realized, apart from being hungry, his tightly wound nerves had turned up absent for roll call, his usual lethargy had vanished, and he had a bounce in his step as he headed to the bathroom to wash up. But as he stood before the toilet to empty his bladder, the sight of the dragon dog tag hanging between his pecs and his freshly shaven pubic area brought everything back, and he had to brace himself or spray the floor. Finished, he turned to the mirror over the sink. He didn't know what he expected to see, maybe lipstick and eyeliner for letting himself be someone's bitch last night?

Always brutally honest with himself, he admitted Sensei hadn't made him feel demeaned in any way, his touch had been.... What?

Orion stiffened his arms on the edge of the sink and hung his head, while he mentally replayed last night's scene in the playroom. The sensei's touch had been caring. Yeah, he'd touched him in places he'd break any other man's arm and all his fingers if he ever tried it but, last night, the touches had not been lewd.

Mind whirling, he leaned closer to the mirror to study his face, reassured to discover his appearance hadn't changed...um, aside from not having any pubic hair. If he kept his clothes on—and he damn sure would—no one, besides himself and his sensei, needed to know about his unconventional choice for rehab.

He grinned ruefully as his stomach told him, again, how much it didn't care about how he'd spent the evening, so Orion stopped picking the scab off his nerves and headed to the kitchen. He hadn't had such a restful sleep in a coon's age. Maybe this small improvement would be enough for now.

Chapter Seven

O ne brief moment of inattention, and his pupil leg-swept him, and put him on his ass. He grinned at the Marine and raised his hand for help up. He chided himself before the class.

"See, even your sensei can be taken down if his mind isn't totally focused on his opponent. But I'm focused now, so why don't we see if you can take me by surprise again."

His class knew what he meant. They would attack in pairs or even in groups while he knelt on the mat. He played fair and looked only at the mat. He didn't want to see whom they chose amongst themselves to attack him. It ended quickly. Dai had the four men on the mat before they knew what hit them, his title of kung fu master secure. He spent the rest of the class going through his moves in slow motion and suggesting ways for his students to counter them.

He enjoyed this advanced class of active duty Marines. He could actually relax with these students because he didn't need to worry about accidentally hurting them if he demonstrated moves above their current level of training. And as had just been demonstrated, they didn't hesitate to push him, either.

As he ate his solitary dinner, Dai contemplated the reason for his inattention. He'd been thinking of Orion Brown, and wondering if he had chosen the right technique for the man. Thus far, he'd seen no full-blown panic attacks, and the shivering he noticed at the beginning of the first session had disappeared by the end of it. The deliberate caress to his cheek and hug good-bye hadn't outwardly disturbed his sub, but Orion hadn't, even as an automatic response, returned the touches.

Dai put his fork down as the realization hit him he hadn't asked Orion to touch him in any manner. Maybe he needed to try that next. Touch and be touched could be a way to desensitize Orion's aversion to using his tactile senses.

Returning his attention to his meal, Dai blinked at the empty plate. He'd eaten an entire meal thinking of Orion Brown and never tasting the food, a sign he needed to get his sub out of his head for this evening.

Grabbing his house keys, he headed out. He'd have a beer at the Irish pub around the corner from the dojo. He knew he'd find some of his pupils or former pupils there who would welcome his presence. Keeping Orion Brown from turning into a hermit didn't necessitate making one of himself.

***

As their instructor, Orion served as observer for the four-man tracker team. Lieutenant Jeremy Barton, the designated tracker, walked in the junction of the Y formation, with the two flankers forming the legs and Captain Jim Parsons, the team leader, walking right behind Barton. Orion slowed his pace after it became obvious Barton lost the spoor. He waited to see what Barton would do next.

"Captain, I've lost the track. We'll have to return to the last positive sign and see if we can pick it up again."

Orion grinned his approval. While a very unpopular decision, due to the North Carolina summer humidity approaching unbearable levels, it told him the lieutenant had been awake during his lecture. He'd just opened his mouth to say as much when Barton, who'd been keeping his focus the correct ten to twenty yards ahead, spun around and promptly torqued his ankle by stepping into an animal burrow. The sudden groan from the Marine lieutenant instantly ruled out a mild sprain, and Orion knelt to assess the damage.

"It's okay, Gunny. I can stand if you help me up."

Orion and Captain Parsons hoisted the lieutenant onto his feet and caught him before his ass could hit the ground again. The lieutenant would not be walking out under his own foot power.

Captain Barton stepped to his side to offer his solution to the problem of getting Lieutenant Barton to the schoolhouse. "If we take it slow and rotate personnel, we can carry Barton between us. It'll take a couple of hours, but we can take frequent rest stops, and I'll bet we reach the compound before it gets dark."

"It's one way to solve the problem, Captain," Orion offered. "But there is another way you can make it easier on the lieutenant and the men. Consider what's around you."

Orion waited until Captain Barton and the team took stock of the pine trees surrounding them.

Not seeing a lightbulb go on in any of the team, he gave them a hint. "How about a Native American solution?"

The lowest ranking member of the team, Sergeant Russell, figured it out.

"You mean a travois, don't you, Gunny? We could cut pine branches and lash them together with our boot laces, and use our packs to form a platform for the lieutenant to lie on. He won't have to hop on one foot the whole time, and it will be easier on the rest of us."

He gave the sergeant a grin and nod of approval, and the team began fashioning a travois. They constructed it with the usual Marine efficiency, and, well before sundown, Lieutenant Barton had his foot tended to by a corpsman.

Orion smoothed over the man's embarrassment before he called it a day.

"You didn't do anything wrong, Lieutenant. You made the right decision to return to where you had a positive sighting of the trail. Even I didn't see that hole under the pine needles. Hazards of walking in the woods, is all. You have the makings of a fine tracker, and I know you'll place your feet more cautiously in the future if you can't see what's under those pine needles."

Orion extended his arm for a shake, but the lieutenant surprised him and pulled him into his chest for a bear hug. He followed the lieutenant's lead and patted him strongly on the back.

He left the team as they joked who would get to be the tracker for tomorrow, now that the lieutenant had figured out a way to get out of losing ten pounds by sweating it out on the trail.

The realization of what he'd done didn't hit him until he dressed for work the next morning. He'd had positive physical contact with one of his students and hadn't freaked out, and he'd slept reasonably well the night before.

Perhaps his choice of BDSM for realigning his psyche would work after all. The delusion lasted until an hour before he had to drive to the Jade Dragon dojo, when he experienced a new version of his panic attack.

For once, he skipped the Afghanistan scenario. This time, doubt crawled like worms through his head and made him clutch the dragon dog tag so hard the chain dug into the back of his neck. His entire body stiffened at the thought of another session with Dai. He didn't want to submit to another man. He sure as hell didn't want to stand docilely bent over a table while a man touched every part of his body, or worse.

Goose bumps running up and down his arms had him scrubbing his skin for warmth, and his addled brain equated the tiny bumps to chicken skin. In a blaze of misguided extrapolation, chicken skin became a euphemism for cowardice. Chicken skin for a chicken. But chickening out would be a stupid reaction since he'd already had some positive results. Yeah, but did these small gains warrant taking this unconventional experiment any farther? How much power over himself must he lose to return to normal?

The recollection of two things got his ass planted on his truck seat to head to the dojo. He remembered the sensei's repeated assurance he had the power of his safe word. He had but to use it, and it would shut everything down faster than a shark could help itself to seconds. The second positive reinforcement occurred in the grocery store.

He'd gone grocery shopping Thursday night because he hadn't anything but peanut butter and stale bread in the house. He'd no sooner put a pound of hamburger and a steak into his grocery cart when someone called his name. He turned around in time to return the hug from the wife of the student whose barbecue he'd ducked out on.

She waved away his apology and followed up with another hug as she laughingly told him she could always tell a bachelor by the meat versus vegetable ratio in their grocery carts. He must have said something clever, for she grinned and patted his arm before wheeling her cart away. He'd finished shopping, gone home, drunk a beer, grilled the steak, and forgotten the whole incident as he took his class to the field the next day.

A good tracker never ignored signs, and Orion Brown saw two very distinct ones. He needed to return to the dojo, and he needed to put on some speed. His dithering came at a cost. He'd be at least five minutes late, which wouldn't endear him to his sensei.

***

With his course of action firmly fixed in his

mind, Dai opened the door to the playroom and gaped at the empty room. No sub waiting in the submissive position. His erect posture slumped. He thought he'd made some inroads—okay, small inroads—into Orion's problem, but perhaps he'd been wrong. The man had chosen not to continue under his tutelage.

Dai turned to leave the room, but stopped when Orion came running from the shower room.

Orion immediately assumed the submissive posture. "I'm sorry, Sensei. I know I'm late, and I have no excuse."

Dai kept censure from his voice. "We will discuss your punishment for the infraction later." He approached his pupil, and, again, caressed the side of his face as he ordered, "Rise."

Orion stood and faced him, and Dai moved to close the gap between them. He maintained eye contact as he pinched Orion's nipples, hard.

Orion's indrawn gasp didn't surprise him. He quickly followed his opening move by bending and taking a now swollen nipple in his mouth and sucking until the bud grew firm. He repeated his actions with the other nipple.

Dai straightened to find blatant sexual excitement, and that truly surprised him. A peculiar feeling fluttered in the pit of his stomach, as he noted Orion's dick stood away from his body with the rigidity of a steel rod. Moira had demonstrated the technique on his own nipples while training him to be a Dom, and for something he never would've considered doing, it had turned him on, instantly. It would seem Orion had the same trigger. He repeated the action to be sure. This time, Orion confirmed his desire for more by pressing his body firmly into his mouth, and Dai gave it to him with lips and tongue before affixing the nipple clamps.

With the lightning reflexes of a kung fu master, Dai scrapped his plan for the evening's play and improvised. If his sub wanted more sensation, he'd get it. Dai walked to the massage table and picked up a black silk scarf.

"Orion, I am going to blindfold you. You'll be able to concentrate on what I am doing to your body. I've started with the nipple clamps, but now I'm going to introduce you to more of the toys used to heighten sensation. Once again, if you feel the need, you may use your safe word, but today's lesson will not involve pain if you follow my instructions. Do you understand?"

Orion gave a hesitant, "Yes, Sensei."

"Lean over the massage table."

Orion complied, and Dai restrained him and picked up a tube of lubricant. Orion clenched his ass cheeks involuntarily as he used a finger to lubricate the crack of his ass, and Dai leaned in and ran his lips along Orion's cheekbone and up to his temple before whispering, "No pain if you follow my instructions. Do not clench. Breathe normally."

Waiting until his sub's breathing returned to normal, Dai began massaging Orion's lower back, buttocks, and the tops of his thighs, until Orion stretched like a cat and squirmed for a more comfortable position. Not having been warned off, he continued with a slow but steady pressure to ease one finger then two into Orion. Once satisfied his sub would accept it, he inserted the smallest of the dildos.

"You are doing fantastic, Orion. Are you

comfortable?"

Dai watched Orion's body closely for small signs of discomfort. The blindfold hid his sub's eyes, so he couldn't see fear or pain in them, and even if he could, he already knew Orion to be very good at schooling his face to hide his emotions.

His sub answered the question with a soft, "Green, Sensei."

Permission given, Dai began inserting and withdrawing the dildo. Orion's shoulders went momentarily rigid but lowered as he became accustomed to the rhythm. A few more strokes and Dai withdrew the plastic rod entirely then lubricated a longer, wider one, and inserted it with hardly a gap in time.

If Orion had not been so adamant about not being touched by another man, Dai would have heightened his enjoyment by reaching around Orion's body to fondle his cock, but he didn't think his sub quite ready for such direct contact between them.

Orion amazed him when he transitioned to the thickest of the dildos and the sub still didn't utter a word of protest or use his safe word. Dai slowed down to consider. Could this be another example of his sub trying to top from the bottom? Dai opened his mouth to inquire, but a deep groan from Orion stopped him.

Dai ceased the in/out motion of the dildo immediately. "Am I hurting you? Do you want me to stop?" Orion answered him not with a word, or a color, but an action. He pushed back, and tilted his hips in the sexual rhythm, an overt demonstration of enjoyment.

Dai didn't trust such a fast capitulation, but he

needed to see how far his sub wanted to take the play, so he calmed his breathing and reached around Orion's hip to gently grasp his penis. Rather than protest or freeze, Orion gave a roll of his hips and began pumping.

An involuntary hiss escaped Dai. He hadn't anticipated such a reaction. He didn't want to reward a demand rather than an acceptance of what he, as the Dom, wanted to grant. Dai quickly brought the exercise to a close by removing the blindfold and the toys.

Dai removed the nipple clips last and blew gently on Orion's nipples to ease the sting of returning circulation. He hesitated at Orion's small mewl of arousal but decided to press on with the script he had originally planned. The time had come for his sub to give as well as receive.

Once Orion tilted his head inquisitively, Dai stripped off the top of his gi. Now that he had his sub's full attention, Dai dropped his pants and stepped, completely nude, out of them. Only then did he turn around to climb up on the massage table. He heard the admiration in Orion's voice as he spoke.

"You're...it's...beautiful. I've never seen anything like it.

*****

As Orion drove home after the session, he felt foolish for having had such hesitation about revisiting the sensei.. Perhaps his imagination had been overly graphic as to what his punishment for being late would be, but whatever Dai had in mind had been delayed until the next session..

As soon as he'd made his lame apology, Dai surprised him by cranking on his nipples until his eyes became unfocused and his dick reacted to the shock like someone had run an electrical current through it. He had never experienced anything like it, but his sexual response felt too damned good to be embarrassed. Having Dai's mouth on his nipples lit him up, and he didn't think he could get any more aroused outside of direct fucking, until the blindfold covered his eyes and the first dildo slid home.

Orion naively assumed this would be all he'd have to endure, until Dai began simulating sex, and Orion amazed himself by getting lost in the movement. His ever-buzzing brain took a leave of absence and left nothing behind but sensory input. His body spoke for his brain as the sensation continued to grow deeper and stronger.

He honestly never even considered rescinding the unspoken permission his body had given the sensei. Orion let it happen and almost came when Dai grasped his dick. He could still hear the groan he gave as the sensei ended the contact and removed the rest of the equipment. Orion didn't make the sound because he'd been hurt. He groaned because he'd been denied. He'd been led to the very edge of orgasm, with his ten toes hanging over the ledge ready to dive headlong into the experience, only to be pushed away from the brink.

Dai hadn't given him a chance to comment or complain but shocked him by stripping off his gi. It forced his brain to re-boot and begin cataloging the signals he'd been sending his Dom.

Orion squirmed at the unfortunate instant replay of how he'd moved his hips, of the moans that signaled his need, and of how he'd used Dai's hand to stroke himself harder.

Orion rocked back as his rational mind began arguing with his libido. One deep part of him had wanted this. The other part diametrically opposed it. Orion forgot his silent argument entirely when Dai turned and exposed his tattoo for the first time.

A dragon. A full-body tattoo of a green dragon. Holy shit, his Dom *was* the Jade Dragon. Orion had never seen such beautiful body art. He almost blurted out something stupid but quickly covered himself by changing "You're beautiful" to "It's beautiful."

He wanted to run his fingers from the tail to the head of the dragon to see if the points of the scales felt as sharp as they looked. The sensei's dragon had been rendered in exquisite artistic detail. It moved as Dai moved, and it rippled whenever Dai's muscles flexed. It made the same inhalation and exhalation as Dai.

The artist had started the point of the wingless dragon's tail below Dai's left ankle, and twisted the tail around his left leg, wound the body across both buttocks and up his spine until the head dropped over Dai's right shoulder to rest on his right pec. The back claws came around his body, right above the deep V of his groin, and the left front claw appeared to grasp his left shoulder, while the right front claw clutched his ribs on the right side.

"It's so perfect, I almost want to pet it," Orion said before he could slap a muzzle on himself.

"And so you shall." Dai gave him a bottle of oil and lay face down on the massage table. "Put your dragon to sleep, Orion."

"M-my dragon?" Orion stuttered.

"I am the Jade Dragon, and you are mine. Inversely, if you are mine, I am yours. This dragon likes long, firm strokes and intensely dislikes tickling."

Yeah, like I'm going to tickle a dragon who could permanently stop my breath with one finger. Orion warmed the oil in his palms and began a long, definitely firm stroke down Dai's back and over the curve of his left buttock. A full body ripple demonstrated the dragon's pleasure.

Thirty minutes into the massage, Orion began to wonder if Dai wanted him to proceed with the front. He stifled a sigh of relief. The sensei chose that moment to sit up and stretch, giving him his answer.

"Thank you, Orion. You give a good massage. Why don't we hit the shower?"

Orion had almost reached the locker room before the use of the word "we" registered. He started to turn around to ask for clarification, but Dai's body slid around his and reached the shower stall ahead of him. Orion watched as Dai adjusted the taps and, when he waved him in, Orion reluctantly stepped into the shower.

Orion discovered his nipples hadn't lost their sensitivity when Dai gently played with them as he soaped his chest. He could feel his dick starting to rise, and he turned into the warm spray to face away from the sensei. Wrong move or right move? Shit, he didn't know at this point, but Dai took it as permission to wash his back and remove all trace of lube from his ass. The sensei believed in thoroughness, and Orion sported a solid boner by the time he started rinsing the shampoo from his hair.

The sensei's ministrations had made him

squeaky clean, so now what? Should he return the favor? Sensei passed him the bar of soap and braced himself on the front wall of the shower. A definite yes then, and Orion soaped up and removed the oil from the dragon. He got caught in a kneeling position after washing the soles of Dai's feet as Dai turned suddenly, putting him at mouth level with Dai's rigid dick.

Orion sucked in a quick breath. It took a monumental effort to raise his eyes to see what the sensei expected of him, and damn if his mouth didn't leap ahead of his brain. He wanted to swallow his foot to choke himself into silence.

"You don't shave your pubic hair."

Orion closed his eyes in mortification and kept them closed. He didn't want to see Sensei's reaction to such an idiotic observation. He opened them only after he felt Dai's calloused palm caress his cheek.

"No, I don't. Would you like me to?"

Orion bit the inside of his lip. Would he? His head made the decision for him by nodding. He would have to analyze this moment later when he lay alone in his bed to see if relief or disappointment won. Dai made no comment but simply turned around to shut the water off.

Once again, Orion dried off quickly and dressed even faster. He watched out of the corner of his eye as Dai dried himself, wrapped the towel around his waist, and walked him to the door to let him out.

Dai stopped in front of the door and didn't speak, and Orion remembered the sensei's parting words from the first session and slowly put his arms around him to give him a brief hug.

Dai's return hug lasted a moment longer than

his.

"I am pleased you remembered, Orion, but this session isn't over for the evening. You have homework."

Dai gave him a small bottle of the oil he'd used on the dragon.

"After you get home, you will strip, get into bed, and call me. I will tell you then what I want you to do."

Orion started to reach for the door but remembered the submissive response in time to murmur, "Yes, Sensei."

"Excellent, Orion. I will be waiting for your call. Oh, and next session, use the stairs to my living quarters. You will not shower first. I haven't forgotten your tardiness today. Good night, Orion. Drive safely."

Orion thought of a number of things he could expect for homework this evening, and none of them could be described as pleasant. His sensei's parting words about his tardiness all but shouted punishment. He wondered if his homework this evening would include pain.

***

He'd been semi erect since Orion left, but the ringing of his cell phone brought on a full hard-on. He answered the call and clicked it to speaker.

"Good evening, Orion. Please put your phone on speaker and rest it on the pillow next to you."

"Yes, Sensei."

Dai waited until the sounds of fumbling stopped then asked, "Have you followed my instructions?"

"Yes, Sensei. I'm, er, undressed and in bed."

"Do you have the oil I gave you?"

"Yes, Sensei."

"Good, pour some into your palm and warm it. You may begin the first stroke if you are ready. You have my permission to vocalize."

"Uh, vocalize, Sensei?"

"You have my permission to express your feelings, Orion. Please begin, but I want you to go slowly and listen to my commands. I will set the pace. You will not come until I give you permission. Do you understand?"

"Yes, Sensei."

Dai began to stroke himself slowly. He closed his eyes and pictured Orion lying on his bed, with one leg bent and his fist around his cock as he stroked himself, and the first tingle of building sexual tension began to firm his sac. "Is the sensation pleasurable, Orion?"

"Yes, Sensei, very."

"Good, increase the pressure, but keep it slow, and make sure to run your thumb over the head."

He followed his own directions for several long, full strokes of his sensitive head. This time he heard a definite breathiness in Orion's "Yes, Sensei," after he commanded him to include the small knot of nerves under the cock's head for the next several strokes.

Dai continued to command his sub, all the while mirroring his actions. Orion didn't know it, but he pleasured himself the same way Dai liked to be stroked. It was taking more and more effort to keep his voice without inflection as he gave the commands. Especially after he'd instructed Orion to use shorter, faster, strokes while fondling his balls.

Orion's sibilant "Yessss," almost set him off, and he returned his attention to his sub.

"Tell me what you are feeling, Orion."

"Honestly, Sensei?"

Dai turned his head on the pillow and grinned at the phone. There'd been a hint of sarcasm, overlaid with a smidgeon of exasperation, in his sub's voice.

"Yes, Orion, I want you to be honest with me. Remember, what we are doing is all about honest communication. I can't help you if you don't tell me exactly how you feel or what makes you feel even better."

"Okay, then. I honestly want to come, Sensei. I can feel it coming. My balls are like rocks, but I'm curious to see what you'll command me to do next. I'm fucking amazed I'm lying here doing this with you listening in. I honestly can't believe only two weeks have passed because, if you'd tried this earlier, I'd have slammed my fist in your face for even suggesting this. Oh, um, let me rephrase. I'd attempt to shove my fist in your face before you made me kiss the dojo floor." Orion groaned. "Sensei, give me another command or give me permission to come because I'm close to imitating Houston Control. The countdown to liftoff is now below four."

Dai's body stiffened at the unexpected revelation. He never thought Orion would lose himself completely in the moment, and listening to his moans made his own orgasm threaten to overwhelm him. He ringed the base of his penis with two fingers and squeezed, hard. He gave the same command to Orion, and heard the hiss as he complied. He waited a ten count before giving the command.

"Now, Orion, stroke hard and fast until you

come. I want to hear you come."

"Yesss, Sensei. Oh shit this feels so good. I'm com.... Ahhh!"

Dai used his pillow to muffle his shout as he came, calling on his martial arts training to return his breathing to normal before he spoke.

"Good night, Orion. Pleasant dreams." Dai ended the call.

Dai sought a comfortable position in bed to wait for the shame to overwhelm him for getting such a kink on, but it never came. Probably because this orgasm exceeded beyond a doubt the perfunctory, taking-care-of-business ones he'd become accustomed to. And from the volume of Orion's shout, he thought it might have been the same for his sub. His introspection lasted only long enough to clean himself up and turn out the light. His brain readily switched off as quickly as the light next to his bed.

Chapter Eight

He almost overslept for work. Orion shaved in haste, adding a few nicks to his face, but he'd be damned if he'd be late. In his entire Marine, and now civilian, career, he'd never been late. For someone accustomed to hearing the slightest noise in the woods, he couldn't believe he'd slept through an alarm buzzing right next to his ear.

His mirror gave further proof this day wouldn't be routine. A wry grin marked a face normally noted for its severe demeanor. Orion had slept like a rock, again, and no way would he berate himself for the means of achieving such a state of relaxation.

The fact their instructor was well rested did not prove to be a boon for the students. Orion kept his class in the woods until sunset. The trail he'd marked for them was a difficult one, but they surprised him with their concentration and ability to find the smallest signs. He permitted himself a brief moment of pride at how fast this class took to tracking. Next week, he'd see if they would be equally as good at disguising their tracks as finding them, especially after he added dogs to the equation.

His students joked with him all the way to the schoolhouse.

"Hey, Gunny, what did you have for breakfast this morning? You look like you rolled out of the sack five minutes ago and not walked through 110 percent humidity for most of today."

Orion laughed at the jibe, but no way in hell would he tell his students his stamina came from Saturday night's spectacularly kinky sex and eight-plus hours of sleep

"I hope you don't leave as many markers next week when you are the ones being tracked," he told them, diverting their attention from his uncharacteristic behavior. "Or it will be as easy to find you as following a herd of elephants. They won't even need to use the dogs."

His teasing had the desired effect, and he and the class traded good-natured insults until they reached the classrooms.

He wished he had a camera to record the expression of astonishment on his students' faces when he accepted their invitation to share a few cold beers at a local bar. Their surprised double takes, followed by their expressions of pleasure, gave him a twinge of regret he'd allowed himself to become withdrawn from these Marines. Maybe having a few beers didn't classify as a big step, but it pointed at least to a positive one. And even if he cringed inwardly at some of the things he'd been doing lately, they did seem to be working.

Orion started to second-guess himself. Maybe he shouldn't have been quite as honest in filling out the

BDSM questionnaire. If he'd fudged a few of his responses, he wouldn't have tested out as such a strong Dom, and maybe the kinky activities he'd been engaging in would have been with Stephanie or Moira rather than Dai.

A hand clapping him on the back abruptly ended his speculation, but not before he realized cheating on the questionnaire might have made his situation worse. He wouldn't have been able to fake being a submissive with a woman. Hell, he barely managed to be one with Dai. The fact Dai could and would kick his ass each and every time his Dominant side tried to take over kept him in line.

"See ya at the bar, Gunny. We hear you're buying the first round."

Orion stunned his class with his response. "Yep, I believe you did, but the last one to get there buys the second round."

The classroom emptied fast, and he laughed all the way to his truck.

***

Orion's good mood, engendered by the last night's camaraderie with his students at the bar, began to wane, as he picked up the keys to his truck in preparation for his weekly session with Dai. His stomach clenched and expressed its unhappiness with not being fed first, or maybe it just wanted to tell him he probably wouldn't enjoy this session. Orion didn't have time to sort out his feelings. He'd earned punishment for being late the last time, and being late again would give Sensei justification to make it harsher.

However, it didn't mean he couldn't devote part of his brain to wondering what the fuck he had gotten himself into as he drove to the dojo. His acceptance of Dai's caresses, of the invasion of his most private recesses, had so jumbled and confused his internal, personal mores he found himself checking the traffic around him to make sure the road was clear for a fast U-turn.

A small voice in the back of his head repeating *You can stop him at any time. You know the sensei will stop with just one word,* kept him headed in the right direction.

Dai parked behind the dojo and had to lean against his truck to take a few deep breaths before he could get moving. Why hadn't he ever used his safe word? He unlocked the door and ran up the stairs, not due to tardiness, but to get away from the answer his libido had just blurted out. He hadn't used it because he hadn't wanted to. Orion didn't want to dig deeper to know the why of it, especially now when the black thoughts, the gut-twisting fears, the mental burden of command responsibilities had started to ease up enough he could be around people and breathe normally.

The clatter of Orion's shoes on the stairs told Dai his sub had arrived. He glanced around the room. Everything was where it needed to be, and he picked up the wrapped bar of unscented soap and moved to meet Orion in the hallway.

It pleased him Orion immediately dropped into the submissive position as soon as he saw him. Dai caressed Orion's cheek and bade him rise.

"Orion, I want you to use this soap for your shower. You may use my bathroom in the master bedroom. When you've finished and dried off, please come to the living room. You may wear a towel if it makes you feel more comfortable."

Dai tilted his head at Orion's failure to respond in the correct manner. His subtle clue prompted Orion to speak.

"I'm sorry, Sensei. Of course I'll follow your instructions. This is the first time I've seen you dressed like, um...."

Dai glanced down at his attire. He'd deliberately chosen to wear traditional Japanese dress. He'd even styled his hair in the traditional bun at the top of his head. He had planned a Japanese punishment for Orion, and he wanted to stay in character. He'd chosen to wear white and brown, from his blindingly white silk undershirt, or *naga-juban*, under his brown-and-white bamboo-patterned *haori* jacket, to the brown-and-white striped *hakama* pants, and his white *tabi* socks.

Orion's blurted comment startled a laugh from him, and Dai grinned, peering down at his sub's feet. He noted Orion hadn't forgotten to remove his own shoes at the doorway.

"You're dressed like a samurai."

Dai bowed and pointed to the door to his bedroom. "Go shower, Orion. I'll be waiting for you in the living room."

When Orion entered the living room, he took his position by the cloth-covered futon. He didn't need to turn around to know the setting confused his sub. All of the furniture had been removed with the exception of the raised mattress. Without moving from his kneeling position, Dai issued orders.

"Remove the towel and lie down on the futon, Orion. You will not speak or show emotion until I give you leave. Your punishment for your tardiness will be what is called *nyotaimori* or body sushi. In essence, you will serve as my plate as I dine this evening."

Dai began placing the artfully rolled pieces of sushi directly on Orion's body. One at the base of his throat, one on each nipple, one on his navel, and one above his pubic area. Satisfied with the arrangement, he poured himself a glass of champagne from the wine bucket he'd placed next to Orion's shoulder.

"Normally, this is a great honor to be used this way. Usually, it's the body of a beautiful woman, but the Yakuza have also used it on men to punish one of their members."

Dai leaned over and used his tongue to delicately scoop the roll from Orion's throat. He finished chewing then took a sip of champagne before speaking again.

"In case you are unfamiliar with the term 'Yakuza,'" he said in a calm voice, "it is the equivalent of the mafia here. They are into moneylending, prostitution, drug and people running. Bad characters, generally. I suspect my stepbrother and my stepfather have Yakuza connections. It is not worth my life to ask them if this is true, but I do know my mother is loved and well cared for by my stepfather. My stepbrother took me to a male body sushi punishment right after he introduced me to the tattoo artist who did the Jade Dragon for me. Yakuza are quite proud of their body art. My stepbrother has a full-body tattoo of a blue demon."

Dai chuckled. "When my mother saw my new decoration, she insisted I be sent away to college in the United States. She didn't want me to lose my American self, so she sent me to UCLA where I majored in languages. I now speak English, Japanese, Chinese, Russian, and French. For a time I worked as an interpreter for ICE, or Immigration, in San Francisco, but I got bored with a nine-to-five job. My love has always been martial arts."

Dai once again leaned down and used a lavish swipe of his tongue to remove a roll from Orion's nipple. His lips twitched in amusement as the nipple pebbled and stood erect, and his sub tightened the muscles in his face to keep from making a sound or showing emotion. He swallowed the roll and had another sip of champagne. He normally didn't drink champagne, but body sushi tradition called for it. He would have been happier with plum wine.

"As I've told you, my father, a Marine, got killed in a training accident. I was only six, but by then I had already won my first competition in Okinawan tae kwan do. My mother recognized my talent and my love of the art, and after we returned to Japan, she sought out the best instructors for me. It was fortunate she did, for I had a difficult time being accepted into the small town my mother called home. She'd left home right after graduating from a business school and got a job as a Japanese translator on Okinawa. She met and married my father and became a naturalized American with dual citizenship. After my father died, she returned home only to discover her parents had been declared missing in an earthquake.

"While searching for her parents, my mother ran

into the old boyfriend who would become my future stepfather. They ran into each other at a hospital. He offered her comfort when she learned her parents had become casualties. He, too, had been searching for his loved ones. His wife had been admitted but succumbed to her injuries, but his son, miraculously, survived untouched. My mother and stepfather had been high school sweethearts who grew apart when he went to university. They renewed their relationship and combined families, but I soon discovered I would have a difficult time fitting in. Japan didn't exactly welcome me with open arms, but my prowess in martial arts, especially tae kwan do, eventually brought me acceptance."

Dai wiped his mouth and took a small sip of wine before leaning over, and, instead of helping himself to more sushi, covered Orion's exposed nipple with his mouth and sucked hard. He permitted a small smile to show on his face when Orion made no sound or movement. He wouldn't fault his sub for the involuntary rise of his penis. He'd expected the reaction. He laved the hurt away and blew gently on the nipple before sampling the sushi on the remaining nipple.

"By the time I reached seventeen, I'd won every competition I'd entered. I wish I could say it didn't go to my head, but it did. I even had the temerity to challenge my stepfather's authority, and he quickly let me know who held the real power in the house. He used his, um, business connections to get me accepted into a Chinese monastery. A monastery noted for the number of Kung Fu Masters it produced. I spent the next eleven years learning kung fu. Somewhere along the line, I lost my false pride and my rebelliousness. I also left there a kung fu master.

"I've already told you I attended college after I returned from the monastery. My mother did not want me to go into the family business of gambling. My stepfather and brother have large interests in several international casinos. I think it's why I got into China without difficulty. My mother surprised everyone by revealing she'd saved every penny of the survivor's benefits she received from the Marine Corps. She'd saved it to use for college, and whatever I wanted after I graduated. I used it to open the Green Dragon Dojo."

Dai once again concentrated on Orion's nipple by sucking hard and twirling his tongue around the hardened nub. He didn't fail to notice Orion swallow hard as he blew on the nipple.

"After San Francisco, I came to North Carolina because one of my friends, a former Marine, told me I should teach special forces Marines and open a dojo near Camp Pendleton or Camp Lejeune. By then I'd been in California for five years and knew what it would cost to open a dojo in that state. North Carolina offered much better real estate prices, and, voila, I opened my dojo in downtown Jacksonville."

The next to last piece of sushi sat on Orion's navel, and Dai circled it with his tongue before claiming it. He then poured a small amount of champagne into the small hollow and enjoyed lapping up the liquid from the unusual cup. Orion had his eyes closed, which made his wide grin go unnoticed. He had to admire his sub; he was remarkably strong in keeping his emotions under control.

He contemplated the last piece of sushi remaining on Orion's body. During the course of the meal, Orion had become sexually aroused. Even though completely full, Dai wouldn't leave his favorite yellow fin tuna untasted. However, the head of Orion's cock rested on the rice and seaweed roll. Undaunted by the challenge, he slowly ran his tongue up the length of Orion's cock. He turned his head at the last minute and took the sushi roll into his mouth. Orion remained rigid until he straightened with the roll in his mouth. He kept Orion waiting while he drained the remaining champagne in his glass.

"You may sit up, Orion. Your punishment is over."

"Yes, Sensei."

"Have you eaten this evening, Orion?"

"No, Sensei."

Orion sat up, and Dai moved onto the futon and patted his lap. "Place your head here, Orion. It will be my pleasure to feed you this evening." And so he did, piece by piece. He lifted his sub's head and helped him drink from the champagne glass.

When Orion refused another piece of sushi, Dai scanned his face as he smoothed the hair from his sub's brow while he deliberated with himself. When Orion didn't attempt to rise at his prolonged silence, Dai smiled down at him.

"Do you know what I'm in the mood for, Orion?"

"No, Sensei."

"I'm in the mood for dessert. The question is, will you surrender and enjoy it with me, or will you use your safe word?"

Since Orion hadn't immediately fled from his

lap, it encouraged him to return Orion's head to the futon and move between his legs.

"You only have to speak one word and I will stop, Orion. Feel free to enjoy this. I don't mind sharing the pleasure."

Dai never broke eye contact as he leaned down and took Orion into his mouth. He listened very carefully for a protest, but only an indrawn breath and a rustle of fabric as Orion clutched the futon, broke the silence in the room.

He moved very slowly at first. He wanted to savor the moment. The salty taste of Orion's skin and the velvet smoothness of the head as he swirled his tongue over it excited him.

Never having done this to another man, Dai flashed to the times a woman had taken him thusly, and simply repeated the techniques he'd enjoyed. He returned to awareness when Orion groaned and moved to rise up on his elbows.

Dai flicked his gaze to his sub and found Orion watching him. His face had thinned out in tension, and his hips were beginning to move in the sexual rhythm.

The expression on Orion's face made Dai's heart beat faster. It had become very warm in the room, perhaps from the champagne he'd consumed. To avoid thinking about what his heated skin might signify, he concentrated on using more suction.

Orion broke the silence with a gasp. "Sensei, this feels extremely good, but I'm not going to last much longer if you keep doing what you are doing."

Dai acceded to his sub's request. This dessert didn't deserve to be consumed too quickly. To give Orion another sensation to concentrate on, he began circling his anus with one finger. Orion neither made an objection or used his safe word, so Dai inserted one finger then two and synced the rhythm with his mouth.

"Ahh, Sensei, please, I'm close. If you don't want me to fill your mouth.... Kenjiiii, oh God, Kenjii!"

Dai drank Orion down then removed his lips when his sub relaxed his body. He crawled up on the futon to join his sub, and Orion astounded him by turning into his body and flinging an arm over his chest.

After granting Orion permission to shower, Dai's mind worked furiously to comprehend what he'd learned this evening. Orion's use of his given name as he came and his affectionate snuggling after tied a knot in Dai's psyche. He'd been playing with fire and had third-degree burns as proof. He thought he'd comprehended what a sub's surrender would mean to him, but he'd been wrong. Now he had a hunger in him, and he ached with it.

Orion returned dressed for the street, and, without a word, Dai walked downstairs with him and opened the door. While pleased his sub actually initiated the hug, he didn't remark on it.

"Orion, you need to consider how much further you want me to take this. I have been nothing but honest with you, and I know you have tried to be honest with me. So I must tell you, if we continue in this fashion, I am going to demand your complete surrender. I don't do things by halves. Tonight, I gave you a faint demonstration of how you could feel if you put yourself completely in my control, but it could be much more. I want it to be more, but if you don't, we end this." His eyes went to where Orion clutched his dragon dog tag in his fist. "If you want to end this now, I will understand. Just remove the pendant and return it to me."

Orion's hand tightened on his dog tag. "Do I have to make a decision tonight, Sensei? I want to think about this. I'll give you my answer at the next session."

And his sub left him speechless with nothing left to do but close the door and listen to Orion's truck rumble down the alley behind his building. Snapping out of it, Dai ran up the steps and straight into the shower. He needed a drink, and champagne wouldn't do. Hell, he didn't think an entire barrel of bourbon would do. He also needed not to be alone with his thoughts.

Some samurai you are, he chided himself as he grabbed his helmet and keys, locked his door, and mounted his bike to head to a bar he knew would be crowded at this time of night.

Chapter Nine

Orion pulled his cell phone out of its holder on his waist with a clumsy fumble. He scrolled through his contact list to hit the number he wanted and waited until someone picked up.

"Hello, Orion. How may I help you?"

"Oh, um, hello, Moira, er, ma'am. You said I could contact you if I needed to speak with you." If he didn't have such good control, Orion would've smacked himself in the head. One glance at the clock on the dashboard told him polite calling hours had ended long ago. "I'm sorry, I guess I should have paid attention to the time before calling you. I'll call you tomorrow. I hope I didn't wake you."

Moira chuckled. "The dungeon keeps late hours, Orion. Now, what has upset you?"

He bit his bottom lip as he pondered how to begin. He must have taken too long to reply, for Moira spoke again.

"Begin at the beginning, or, better yet, why don't you come here for a face-to-face?"

"Yes, ma'am. When would be convenient?"

"As you are still up and wide awake, how about right now? I've seen my last client for the evening, and I can give you my exclusive attention."

"Excellent, ma'am. I'm on my way home from Jacksonville. I can be there in under an hour. Are you sure you don't mind seeing me?"

"I'll always make time for you, Orion. I'm assuming this has something to do with your Dom."

"Yes, ma'am, it does."

"Okay, then. I'll be waiting, but you need to do something for me first."

"Yes, ma'am. What do you want me to do?"

Orion fervently hoped Moira wouldn't order him to strip nude and assume a submissive pose after entering The Willows. Dai had already sensitized his skin enough for one night. Dai's ghost touch still stroked, and his mouth continued to lick sensitive places on his body. And that was what bothered him. How in the hell had he gone from frozen to incendiary in such a short space of time? Moira was the only one he knew who wouldn't hold him in contempt or think him a sick son of a bitch for discussing his feelings.

Moira's voice drew him back.

"Orion, you can stop calling me 'ma'am.' If you must give me a title, you can use Mistress or Madame or, better yet, Moira. Drive carefully. I'll tell Stephanie to bring you directly to my office when you get here."

After Moira ended the call, the silence in his truck weighed heavily, and Orion hurriedly turned on the radio. Right now, having quiet surround him so he could ponder the day's events didn't appeal at all.

In fact, the country and western station playing unrequited love ballads made his gut churn.

Much better, he thought, as he hit on a station playing rap. He couldn't understand half the words, but the coarse language and hard beat kept him from being able to think of anything but driving.

His ears thanked him as he pulled into The Willows and turned the music off. He could only gawp wordlessly when Stephanie greeted him at the door. Her demur dress and pearls had been replaced by female fetish-wear. He didn't know if the sparkly collar she wore sported diamonds or rhinestones, but he now knew Stephanie was a sub. He at least found his vocal cords in time to thank her before she opened the door to Moira's office for him. He lost them again as Moira walked into his line of sight. She wore an emerald-green leather bustier and pencil skirt with matching open-toed stiletto heels. No need to ask Moira if she subbed or dominated. The one-tailed whip she tossed onto her desk said it all.

His toes curled in his sneakers as he looked down at his worn jeans, and he apologized for his casual attire.

"Orion, there's no need to apologize. While I like a man in a well-cut suit, I know you didn't plan on being here tonight. Have a seat. I've ended my day with a long-standing client, and I've worked up a thirst. Will you join me in a scotch?"

Orion nodded. He still needed to put a BOLO out on his voice box and maybe an APB on his brain after watching Moira cross her long, long legs. The coral paint on her toes drew his eyes. Moira's cocky grin told him she'd noticed where he'd been staring. Damn, he needed to give up playing poker or he'd be broke for the remainder of his life.

Orion gave her silent kudus for recognizing the moment he went from brittle to simply nervous, but she didn't let him maintain his silence for long. The Willows' Mistress got down to business by pointing out the elephant hogging space in her office.

"I won't say I'm surprised to see you again, but I will say I'm surprised it took you this long. Tell me, Orion. I'll help you any way I can, but you mustn't prevaricate."

Once again, the Great Spirit helped him out of a jam. Stephanie entered with the liquor tray, giving him a chance to delay his response while Moira busied herself playing hostess. She didn't bother asking him how he liked his drink but fixed his preference and poured one for herself.

Orion watched Moira watching him for approximately a nanosecond before blurting, "I want him...completely."

The bald admission horrified him. He hadn't planned on saying it...*ever*. He had no idea why he'd said it now, but it couldn't be recalled.

Moira leaned forward and patted his knee, which encouraged his mouth to continue spewing.

"I'm not a.... I don't.... I've never...." Damn, somewhere between Jacksonville and Wilmington he'd truly lost his brain.

Orion began to think he should start casting around Moira's office for tracks leading to the yellow brick road because he obviously needed to find Oz and help himself to a new brain.

"Let me fill in those blanks for you," she said. "You're not a homosexual. You don't have sexual relations with men. You've never had these feelings before. Have I gotten it right?"

It had been a rhetorical question, so he kept his mouth shut.

"Orion, what you want is not Kenji's body as much as you want to surrender all of you to Kenji. You are a pragmatic man, Sky Hunter Brown. If some of something is good, then more of the something is better. You have amazed yourself with how fast you have surrendered even this much of your will to your Dom, and it has confused and frightened you, but I don't think it has frightened you enough to keep you from seeing it through, or am I wrong?"

"No, no, Moira, you are not wrong. Ever since I let Dai...let Dai touch me, I've...ached. I've ached to surrender, to fall off the cliff and leave these fears behind, and I am beginning to trust Dai enough to let him catch me when I fall." Orion slumped in his chair. "But I can't help thinking it's wrong. Does a real man surrender to another man?"

Moira steepled her fingers under her chin and studied him a moment before speaking.

"I think what you want to know is, does surrendering make you a homosexual? No, it does not. What you are is a warrior who has had little contact with women. You spend your days entirely in the company of men. You admire men. Oh, I'm not speaking only of their physical attributes. In fact, I doubt you actually pay attention to their bodies. You admire and are attracted to their spirit, their strength, their courage.

"As a Native American, you have tribe built into your genes. You mentioned you weren't raised on a reservation, but I think you've substituted the Marine Corps for your tribe. But admiring men doesn't mean you have no appreciation for women, Orion. You like women, and I doubt you've had any difficulty bedding them. But let's be honest here, has there been any woman who's stood out in your mind? Have you ever had so great an itch to copulate with her it overrode your common sense?"

Orion didn't respond, and Moira patted his knee.

"In and of itself, not having frequent sexual congress with women doesn't make you a homosexual. It possibly makes you a bisexual. You are not unique. Many overly alpha men can be bisexual.

"Your Dom has shown you a side of yourself you weren't aware existed. Is it wrong to surrender your body to his Dominance? I'd say no, it isn't, but I'm not an overly rigid, religious person. What I am is a student of history. The greatest armies in the world had warriors who preferred men to women, but it didn't affect their performance, and it certainly didn't mean they showed up for battle dressed in heels and lipstick. Actually, I've found such overly masculine men to be quite pragmatic about seeking release from their testosterone overload. The fact Dai's power turns you on is simply a sign you've turned a corner in your healing. You are not as frozen as you once were."

Moira reached out and caressed Orion's cheek to center his attention.

"Orion, I want you to close your eyes and think of Dai. Tell me what you see."

Orion remained silent as he gathered his thoughts. "I see a warrior. You can tell by the balanced way he stands. It isn't something he does deliberately, but it's natural for him.

"He appreciates order and symmetry. His living quarters reflect this. He doesn't put on airs. He is usually the first to laugh at himself if something goes wrong, but he is considerate of other people's feelings. He has a compassionate nature. When he cares for me after a session, I never get the feeling he is just going through the motions to get me the hell out of there.

"He's trustworthy. I know if I ever used my safe word, he would stop immediately and talk it over with me until he understood why I didn't like it."

Moira nodded her head, approvingly. "Good, Orion, but now I want you to go a little deeper. Tell me how you feel about him."

Orion wet his lips and broke the silence. He spoke from his heart. "He's beautiful. His body is a work of art, literally. The green dragon is part of him. It breathes and moves as part of his body.

"He is handsome for a man. His eyes are astounding. Green eyes in an Oriental face draw everyone's attention, but I like the fact he isn't aware of it.

"He's built like a warrior. Not an ounce of fat. Defined muscles, broad shoulders, straight posture. He exudes strength. You sense he can crush you with a flick of his wrist, but his touch is gentle."

Orion took a deep breath and rushed the next sentence. "When he caresses my face each time he brings me out of the submissive pose, I want him. I want him to hold me, to take me. His hands are rough, not soft. He has calluses like I do from hard work at his craft. I like the feel of them rasping over my skin.

"He seems to know intuitively what turns me on.

Whenever he pinches my nipples, it is very hard for me not to orgasm, but I get ashamed by responding so physically."

Moira interrupted his confession.

"Do you think Dai is impervious to your reaction? Do you think it turns him off?"

Moira's question took him by surprise. "Until tonight I had no clue what Dai thought, but tonight he...he...."

Orion covered his face until Moira reached over and gently tapped him on the knee.

"No, Orion, no avoiding the question. Tell me what happened tonight. What did Dai do or say to upset you enough to come here?"

Orion moved to the edge of his chair and accepted Moira's caress of comfort.

"He went down on me. He allowed me to come in his mouth then he drank me down. Afterward, he walked me to the door and let me go home."

Moira shook her head as a confused expression crossed her face. "The abrupt parting doesn't sound like Dai. Wham, bam, and don't let the door hit you in the derriere, doesn't sound like the Dai I know."

Orion abruptly shifted deeper into his seat. "No, no it isn't. I didn't mean to give that impression. He did feed me, and cuddle with me, and ask me how I felt. I called you because of what he said right before I left. He told me I needed to think about whether our Dom/sub relationship should continue because, if we continued, he would take me."

Moira's eyes never left his, as she asked, "Take you? Can you be more specific on what he meant?"

Orion massaged his right eyebrow but stopped in mid-motion. "He wanted my complete sexual submission. No more him getting me off. It would be a complete union. He wanted reciprocity. Tit for tat or dick for ball, if you don't mind my being crude."

"And this offended you?"

Orion winced at the question.

"Offend? No, it didn't offend me, Moira, it excited me, and I couldn't deal with it. I told him I'd let him know at the next session, but I'm not sure I won't chicken out by then. I wish to God I could say he hasn't helped me at all, but he has. I sleep better, I work better, I'm a better person to be around, and it's all because my Dom has done things to my body no man ever has, and I'd be lying if I said it didn't scare me shitless."

"You shouldn't be frightened at all. Orion, you see more than most people ever do, and what you've seen is your Dom's power. You admire it, and you are human enough to want to be protected by it, but you are forgetting one thing. You are not powerless. It is you, the sub, who will be the one to decide if he receives your submission. It is you who have the power of the safe word. One little word spoken aloud, and, as much as your Dom wants your complete surrender, he doesn't get it."

Orion tried to speak, but Moira held a finger up and stopped him.

"The English statesman, Edmund Burke, once said, 'No passion so effectually robs the mind of all its powers of action and reasoning as fear.' You have a week to think about this. My advice to you is, don't let your fear keep you from acting on what your heart is telling you it wants."

Moira rose from her chair, and he did as well. She opened her arms for a hug.

"Good night, Orion. We both know I can't make the decision for you, but I know you are accustomed to listening to your own good counsel, and not what other men say you should do or think or feel. I also know, whatever you decide, it will be based on sound deliberation. I wish you well."

Until he returned to his truck and the scent of expensive perfume wafted through the cab, Orion didn't realize he'd actually hugged the beautiful Dominatrix. Damn, Dai had done it. Three weeks ago, no way in hell he would've hugged any woman, least of all such a sexy woman, without coming unglued.

A sudden jaw-cracking yawn overtook him, and he slumped with fatigue. He doubted he would be awake long enough to count stars through his skylight this evening.

***

Dai deliberately chose a different bar from his regular. The Irish pub he usually frequented leaned toward being a family bar, and, with the thoughts banging around in his head, Dai didn't want to stand shoulder to shoulder with wives and kiddies ordering fries and chicken nuggets. He wanted hard-drinking, silent, mind-your-own-fucking-business drinking companions.

He ordered beer with a whiskey back for starters as he bellied up to the bar. He'd been sitting Japanese fashion most of the evening, and standing let him stretch his back muscles. He tossed down the shot and had taken a healthy swig of his beer when someone called his name.

Great, a former student. Sometimes he wished

his Oriental manners would take a vacation, so he could be as rude as any Westerner who wanted to be left the hell alone.

He resigned himself to small talk and politely returned the man's greeting. Both of their attentions were caught by the bartender refusing to serve two men to Dai's left.

"Sorry, sir, I'm not serving you another drink. You've had four in the last hour. I'd ask your friend here to drive you home, but he's had as much as you. I can call you a cab. We have a no-fee service for our customers who don't want to risk a DUI."

Rather than accept the bartender's suggestion, the man turned and pointed at Dai. "You won't serve me, a red-blooded American, but you'll serve the chink?"

Dai's student swore under his breath and slammed his glass on the bar. Before he could move, Dai grabbed him on the shoulder and shook his head.

"Don't. The man is obviously three sheets to the wind and doesn't know what he's saying. It's not worth showing up on the General's Monday Morning Blotter for being arrested for brawling."

To Dai's chagrin, the man may have been inebriated, but his hearing hadn't been affected by the alcohol.

"Three sheets to the wind?" he railed, his volume turned up. "I'm as sober as you are, chink. Americans can hold their liquor better than squinty-eyed slopes."

Dai gritted his teeth but kept any expression of annoyance from his face. "You are mistaken if you think I am Chinese. I am not a chink or a slope. I am, in fact, Japanese-American."

The drunk brought his silent friend into the discussion. "Huh, Charlie, he says he's American, but ain't no American man I know wears his hair in a *bun*, unless he's a fag. You a fag, Mister Jap?"

Ah, shit. In his haste to escape serious soul searching, he'd forgotten he'd styled his hair in the traditional way. No way would he explain Japanese customs to this bigoted drunk.

"Listen here, buster," the bartender cut in, "you need to take yourself and your friend out of this bar. See this?" He held up a baseball bat and a cell phone. "One more word and I'm hitting 911 and calling the police. If you even think of taking a swing in here, I'm going to get some batting practice in. Now, get the hell out of here and go find someplace else to start a fight."

It looked like the bartender had defused things when the men pushed away from the bar.

"You're lucky you made the right decision, pal," Dai's former student taunted. "The man you insulted could wipe the floor with you with one hand tied behind him."

Dai swore silently in Japanese.

The man walked up to him, grabbed his beer, and chugged it. He smirked at Dai as he wiped the foam from his lips. "Well, Mister Jap fag, why don't we step behind this bar and see if you really can wipe the floor with me. I promise to not mess up your hairdo. If you ask me nicely, I might not split your lip so you can kiss your friend here good night."

Dai once again had to restrain his former student. Resigned, he turned to the bartender who still held the bat and phone. "I don't believe the bat will be necessary, but you might want to dial 911."

"You want me to call the cops?"

"No, sir, I think you should call an ambulance."

Dai gestured for the man to lead the way then placed a twenty dollar bill on the bar to pay for his beer and shot. "Keep the change for the inconvenience I seem to have caused this evening."

The alley behind the bar glowed brightly with security lights. Not for the first time, Dai wondered how the word of a fight could spread so fast without an actual announcement. He waited patiently and sized his opponent up while the man postured for the uninvited crowd.

Dai noted the man had about fifty pounds on him. Um, more like fifty-five, if he included the heavy biker boots. He also had longer arms, but it didn't matter. The man had had too much to drink, and it would slow his reflexes. He wished his honor didn't demand he let the man make first contact. His training made it imperative he defend himself, not initiate the fight.

He mentally prepared himself for the pain of a fist striking his face. Dai shook his head ruefully, and it dawned on him maybe he'd been seeking such a confrontation all evening. Nothing like a good fist in the face to get your head on straight.

He kept his arms crossed and his feet planted as the man taunted him with short jabs as if shadow-boxing.

"Are you going to fight me, fag, or do you want to be my bitch for the evening?"

For the first time since he'd walked into the bar, Dai permitted a smile to appear on his face. "You want me to kiss you? Sorry, not going to happen unless I do it with my fist. Now, stop that clumsy footwork and take your best shot. You're only going to get one."

As he knew it would, the insult worked, and a meaty fist connected with his prominent cheekbone. Damn, the man's large ring tore a chunk out of his cheek.

With honor assuaged and first blood drawn, Dai effortlessly put the man down with a backhand strike to the sweet spot right above where the jaw connected. The obnoxious drunk went down like a sack of concrete to sprawl flat on his back in the dirt. He would not be insulting anyone else for the rest of the night.

"Hey, I'm not going to let you get away with sucker-punching my friend."

Dai had plenty of time to send Charlie sailing with a push kick. Charlie had intended to even the score by using the large brick that had propped the exit door open, but Dai's kick slammed him into the wall and flung the brick into the air. Unfortunately for Charlie, it landed on his crotch after he slid down the wall and took a seat. Charlie immediately forgot about defending his friend's honor in favor of cradling his jewels and dry heaving.

"Okay, break it up. Everyone who hasn't thrown a punch, either leave or go inside. The fight's over."

Dai shook his head at the policeman's command. The bartender had called 911. He didn't know if the champagne he'd imbibed earlier had caused his headache or his head throbbed because he felt foolish for brawling. The sensation of blood running down his check caught his attention. Dai took his handkerchief out and held it to his face.

"Sensei, I didn't expect to find you involved in

this."

Dai's headache increased. Damn, another former student, and this one a policeman. Before he could explain, his over-eager former student spoke up and pointed to the drunk who hadn't moved from where Dai planted him.

"The sensei didn't start the fight. This man insulted him with racial slurs and then punched him. And his buddy tried to crack the sensei's skull with a brick when he had his back turned, but the sensei kicked him into the wall, and the brick somehow landed on his junk. I hope he sings soprano for the rest of his life for fighting dirty."

"Is he telling the truth, Sensei?"

"Yes. I tried to avoid fighting them. I didn't hurt them as much as redirect their aggression into the contemplation of the negative effects of alcohol abuse."

The cop started laughing. "Oh that's rich, Sensei. The contemplation of alcohol abuse. Oh good, here are the paramedics. Why don't we let them see to your face? It's bleeding pretty good. You might need stitches. I'm surprised the guy actually tagged you."

"The man didn't tag the sensei," the former student said, once again leaping to his sensei's defense. "The sensei let him have the first shot. He didn't even try to avoid the haymaker, but he sure as fuck ended it."

Dai turned and watched as the paramedics worked on his opponents. It didn't take them long to declare both in no danger of dying, except maybe from cirrhosis. One of the paramedics made Dai hold still to clean and dress his cut with some butterfly bandages, and he cast his eyes down in embarrassment.

"I don't think you'll even have a scar from this. The cut isn't too deep. The butterflies will hold it. If you start noticing any redness or swelling or a yellow discharge, go to your doctor and have him examine it."

Dai thanked the paramedic and headed home after the cop completed the required paperwork. He dragged himself slowly up, step by step, to his living quarters. He'd wanted oblivion and gotten remorse. Before he showered off the dregs of his bad decision to go to the bar, Dai texted Moira and asked for a meeting in the morning. Maybe she would have some insightful suggestions he could act upon instead of fighting with strangers.

***

Moira watched Dai walk toward her as she sat behind her desk. The man walked like a stalking panther, the black, tropical wool suit accentuating his broad shoulders, narrow waist, and long legs. The man exuded power, and the cut on his cheek only added to the don't-fuck-with-me vibe he gave off.

She'd seldom seen Dai show any emotion other than cheerfulness, and the devil in her didn't want to make this easy on him. The fleeting thought this powerful Dom might throw her over her own desk and take her to teach her a lesson for messing with him sent shivers down her body and made her core wet with interest.

Moira stood and moved to take a seat in one of the wing chairs, and Dai failed to react to her dress, a severely cut sapphire-blue linen sheath without the slightest ornamentation except for the thigh-high slit. She also wore sapphire earrings and a sapphire bracelet, but even the large blue gems didn't catch his interest, and neither did the matching stilettos. Dai's non-reaction to such visual stimulation told her the sensei wouldn't be as easy to convince as Orion. Moira did note Dai, despite being visibly upset, hadn't forgotten his manners. He'd remained standing until she seated herself.

"Did you know your sub came to see me last night?" As she knew she would, Moira startled Dai with her opening sentence.

"Tell me how you knew when I didn't even know?"

Moira noted Dai's jade eyes snapped with anger as he asked the question but had quickly morphed into something closer to shame. His reaction disturbed her. She knew what he asked, even if his wording hadn't broached the topic directly. She stalled to buy time to formulate an answer he would accept.

Moira pressed the buzzer under her table. "I think this calls for a nice pot of jasmine tea. The explanation will take some time and a bit of a confession from me. But while we wait for Stephanie to bring it, why don't you tell me how you hurt yourself."

Dai started to touch his face and stopped. "I had to give a drunk a lesson in manners."

"Is that true, Sensei? I thought your training preached avoiding fights."

"It is, and I did try, but sometimes your opponent forces the issue."

"And sometimes you need a good fight to get rid

of some excess testosterone."

Stephanie entered with the teapot and two paper-thin porcelain cups, and Moira laughed outright at the wall-to-wall relief on Dai's face for not having to respond to her jibe.

"Thank you, Stephanie. I'll play mother."

Moira poured the tea and passed a cup to Dai. She knew he took it without sugar, as did she. She waited until Dai sampled his beverage before resuming their conversation.

"I suppose I should start with the confession." Now she had the full attention of two beautiful jade orbs.

"It's true, my name is Moira Cavendish, but it is also Doctor Moira Cavendish. I am a fully licensed psychologist. I had a marriage counseling practice in Silicon Valley before coming to North Carolina."

"Why did you leave?"

Moira crossed her legs and arranged her dress, the better to display one of her best features. Ah, Dai had calmed enough to notice the maneuver.

"I left because the rich, neurotic, spoiled, insensitive people I called clients failed to understand they didn't need a larger house, another child, or a better body to fix their marital discord. They did need to open their ears and listen to each other, but they refused to listen to such a simplistic solution to their angst, and so the marriages dissolved in spectacular, greedy divorces.

"And what a shame. It soon became obvious to me what they really needed was a good spanking and then to be put to bed and cuddled, but I couldn't reach them. These people put so much effort into acquiring status symbols as measures of their worth, they lost the capacity to feel, to touch and be touched.

"I ranted about this to a colleague of mine, and he shocked me by admitting he'd become a practicing Dom, and spanking did get people to focus. He initiated me into the BDSM world, and it seemed logical to connect psychological counseling to the therapeutic properties of BDSM.

"It took me a year to develop the online questionnaire I use here. Yes, it does tell me whether or not the person is a Dominant or a submissive, but it also tells me what their fears are, and what they are seeking by applying for membership in The Willows.

"I take extreme care in matching the Dom/sub partners, for what would be the point of randomly assigning the next available person to a new client if he or she couldn't give or get what they needed? I sincerely want to help people, and I can tell it's working. Our membership is stable, and the feedback is positive."

"Is this what you did with Orion and me?"

Moira didn't even try to beat around the bush. "Yes, yes it is. You and Orion are very unusual in your psychological makeups. I always searched for a sub for you, in case you ever wanted to play in the BDSM arena, but until Orion came along, no one suited. Orion had the same difficulty in finding a partner to help him. You and only you complemented his needs and desires."

Dai burst from his seat. "I shouldn't think it hard to match two homosexuals."

Moira put her cup down with a distinct clack. "Kenji, neither you nor Orion is homosexual. If a label must be put on you, try bisexual. If I had to name it, I'd simply say you and Orion are supremely compatible, even though you are both alpha males. Neither one of you has a submissive bone in your body, but you are compassionate men who have no trouble switching roles if it helps your chosen partner."

Moira held both of her arms out to Dai and kept them extended until he knelt to accept the comfort of her embrace.

"Kenji, you've spent most of your life with men. You've taught them, encouraged them, and most of your day is spent in their company. I'm not trying to point out the obvious by saying you like women, but can you even remember the last time you consciously sought out a woman to spend a day or a night with?"

He sputtered, but she shushed him.

"No, I don't want an answer to my question. The point I am trying to make is you savor strength not softness.

"Orion is much the same. He spends his entire week teaching Marines how to read the signs of what passed through an area. He, like you, has been blind to the emotional signs in front of him. No woman he's encountered to date has been strong enough to master him. I think your going down on him opened his eyes enough to understand what he wants and needs now."

Moira released Dai. "My advice to you is to explore this with him, but tread softly. He is hyper-observant of everything around him, and he's seen too many bad things. The fact he has willingly submitted to you to this extent and this quickly tells me he sees you as someone he trusts enough to change his focus."

Moira waggled her finger at Dai like a lecturing

parent.

"Now, let's discuss what you want. From the amount of agitation you displayed when you walked in today, I can tell dominating this man has come at some cost to you. You've begun to transfer your natural caring tendencies to Orion, and it has you spooked because you do feel affection, deep affection for him. Would I be wrong to say you are especially upset by the fact you want him and you want him to reciprocate?"

Color rose in Dai's cheeks.

"I did a damn fine job teaching you, Kenji. Rather than being disturbed by Orion's response to you, you should be celebrating. You've had a taste of the ultimate aphrodisiac, a Dom's power over his sub, and now, unconsciously, you want the whole enchilada. You want his complete surrender. And let me add, aside from being my star pupil, you are a precocious one. You also want to feel what a sub feels when he gives total control to someone he trusts, someone he loves enough to willingly sublimate his own will."

Dai interrupted, "Isn't that what I did with you?"

Moira gave Dai's cheek a playful pinch. "No, you didn't. *Learning* how to be a Dominant by playing the sub is not the same as really being a sub. You never totally surrendered to me, and I never demanded your total surrender." Moira hesitated and tapped her lips with one brightly polished nail. "Hmm, I think I need to remind you a Dom can choose to submit to their sub if it suits him to switch. You've been so busy trying to keep Orion from topping you, you haven't actually called a time out and let him do it for your own pleasure."

Dai resumed his seat. "Did you tell this"—he made a vague gesture encompassing Moira's office— "to Orion?"

"I certainly didn't tell him of my psychology degree, but I did ease some of the same fears you have. You two mirror each other in your reactions, and I'm not going to say anything more. I consider my clients to be patients, and I don't tell tales out of school. If you want to know what Orion thinks, you'll have to ask him."

Dai hung his head and studied the pattern on the Persian carpet before responding. "If I get the chance. I'm not sure I'll ever see him again. I told him, if he returned to the dojo, I would work to take the sex deeper."

Dai pounded his knees with his clenched fists. "This waiting to know what his response will be is killing me, and I know the pressure of my demand probably isn't having a positive effect on Orion. God, I can't believe I even said it. Until you explained it, I had no idea where these feelings sprang from. I hope I haven't led Orion into a corner where he freezes up again. We actually have made good progress in his ability to touch and be touched."

Moira bit her lip as Dai uttered an easily translatable word in Japanese. "Orion will return to you, Dai. Maybe only to return the gauntlet you threw down, but he won't slink away without first telling you exactly how he feels. And you need to make up your mind whether you want to act on your feelings. In my professional opinion, this is something you are telling yourself you need or want right now. Whether or not it becomes a lasting relationship or a D/s one for Saturday nights, I can't say. Only you and Orion will be able to find the answer."

The phone on her desk rang once, and Moira stood. "Ah, my client has arrived. Come here, Dai, and give me a hug."

As Dai came into her arms, Moira scrutinized his face before she spoke.

"You don't know how much I hope you and Orion work things out. You are both good men, and I would see you happy. Now, go and do something fun with the rest of your weekend. Even though this is a Chinese proverb, I offer it for your contemplation. 'Do not engage in needless worry of things you cannot change'. You can't make up Orion's mind for him, so don't spend the week brooding. You'll know what his answer is soon enough."

***

Dai woke early Monday morning but didn't immediately rise. He needed time to contemplate the epiphany he'd had. It had been triggered by something Moira said to him yesterday. Specifically the phrase, "This is something you seem to want now."

Dai's mind, by its own convoluted reasoning, flashed to his years in a Shaolin temple having the principles of compassion beaten into his thick Japanese skull through the slow drip of repetition. He'd wanted to be a kung fu master, and he made the commitment to slow his life down to wake at five thirty every morning, chant for two hours, eat breakfast at seven thirty, followed by a twenty minute study break, a three-hour kung fu training session, lunch at eleven, another hour study break, concentrated study of the Diamond Sutra, another two-hour kung fu session, dinner at five thirty, more chanting of the Heart Sutra for an hour, and, finally, bed at ten p.m. Day in and day out.

No surprises for eleven years to instill discipline. He had to learn discipline before he could learn Buddhism. He needed to understand what *wuchang* or impermanence was. He now knew everything he did every day changed, and passed, and got old. Only by taking life by the moment would he be able to relish each experience, old and new.

Now he needed to taste a man's surrender, to dominate another powerful man and give his care, his concern, his love in return. It would be a new experience for him, and so he needed to slow down and appreciate every moment of it. His temple training had taught him how temporal life could be and that love had to be given, not hoarded, and cherished when reciprocated.

Dai rose from his bed in a much calmer mood. He hoped Orion would find the courage to act on his feelings, and if he did, he would return them. If his sub couldn't find it in him to continue, then Kenji would be grateful he'd been given the honor of knowing Orion Brown and be satisfied with the experience and the knowledge he'd sincerely tried to help him.

Chapter Ten

O rion sat on his deck after work on Monday and stared in the direction of the shrimp boats trawling the New River, but he didn't really see the boats. His damn cell phone, sitting on the deck railing, had captured his attention. The fucking thing had turned into a serpent, an extremely venomous one. It dared him to touch its blank screen and punch in Kenji's number so it could kill him with mortification. Orion knew if he did actually dial the number, his vocal chords would seize up and leave him mute. What could he possibly say? *Hey there, Sensei, how's about you and I spend all next Saturday fucking? You don't even need to tie me up because I'm already hard thinking about you going all dragon on my ass.*

Orion groaned and thunked his head on the deck rail. Such an outrageous thought left as quickly as it came. He wanted something he couldn't define, so how could he possibly explain it to Dai?

It had been so much easier letting his Dom guide him. He didn't have to voice his preference. Oh, he knew not saying his safe word meant he agreed with what Dai did with his body, but he *didn't actually have to say it.*

In his heart of hearts, Orion wanted the status quo to continue ad infinitum, but Dai had given notice last week he didn't find that acceptable. His sensei wanted words, wanted verbal permission to engage in reciprocal sex, and, if he understood him correctly, not simply as part of play or punishment.

For the first time, Orion wished he and Dai had an actual friendship. He wanted to go fishing or kayaking or hang out at a bar or toss a football around, but not with his sensei. He wanted to do those things with Kenji, the man. Shit, did kung fu masters even know how to do those things? He didn't know, and thus his current angst. He had never engaged in casual sex. If he crawled into bed with someone, he wanted to know them a great deal better than carnally.

Oh God, he'd turned into a dithering sissy wondering whether or not he should call his Dom. His cell phone rang and scared the ever-loving piss out of him. It was Dai.

"H-hello?" *Wow! Could I be any lamer in the conversation openers?*

"Hello, Orion. I know you probably didn't expect me to call, but I wanted to apologize for putting pressure on you. If you aren't ready for what I suggested, I'll understand. If you want to continue as we have been, I'll go along. And I will also understand if you want to stop altogether, but...I hope you want to continue because I think you are starting to be more at ease around people."

Before he could stop himself, Orion blurted, "It's

not what I want."

The pregnant silence on the other end clued him in Dai expected him to be a fucking bit more specific.

"Um, I don't want to stop our sessions."

"Okay, I understand. We'll continue as before."

Orion shook his head until he realized, duh, phone not on FaceTime, and hurriedly offered clarification. "I don't want to continue as before. I want to explore your suggestion, but I want more."

This time, the sensei's pause was so long Orion thought he'd lost the connection until Dai spoke again.

"Orion, I am prepared to give you what you want, but you need to be specific here. Are we talking relationship, purely D/s, or some combination of the above?"

"Sensei, I wish I could put it in black and white, but I don't know exactly what I'm asking for except...." *Fuck, this would be so much easier if I could use telepathy.*

"Except what, Orion?"

Orion swallowed convulsively and stepped off the cliff. "I want to be friends. I want us to be friends who have, um, privileges. I want a relationship based on friendship, and trust, and to let it progress and see where it goes. If we are to, uh, have sex outside of the playroom, I don't want it to be fucking for the sake of fucking, Sensei."

He'd fallen into full-babble mode, and he hadn't put on a shirt before going out on the deck. If he had, he'd drag it off now and stuff it in his mouth to stifle himself.

"Okay, I'll be honest and admit, yeah, I probably would enjoy fucking for the sake of fucking, but I want more from you. Am I making any sense, Sensei?"

"Perfect sense. Orion. Aside from our D/s sessions, do you think you could possibly use my given name when we are fucking not for the sake of fucking? Hearing you call my name in passion is a huge turn-on for me."

Orion burst out laughing to hear the sensei parrot his ludicrous phrasing back at him and calmed down enough to reply. "Yes, Kenji, I can. And I would like to hear you call me Sky when we, um, are not in the playroom."

"I am honored you would gift me with your Lakota name. Yes, I will call you Sky. I have to go. I have my last class of the evening about to start."

Now or never, now or never, his brain urged. "Um, Kenji, do you want to go kayaking with me next Sunday?"

"Kayaking? I've never tried it, but I've always wanted to. I don't have a kayak, though."

"Not a problem, I have a two-person one, in addition to my smaller one."

"Then, yes, I'd like to go kayaking with you."

Orion ended the call and promptly started to strip as soon as he left the deck. He'd soaked his underwear and shorts with nervous perspiration. Honest communication between a Dom and sub would take some getting used to, but at least his stomach could begin untying all the knots he'd tied it in.

***

Stephanie's knock on the door found Moira

stretched out on the antique fainting couch in her office. Moira liked the comfortable couch; it had facilitated some memorable performances *a deux*.

"Sorry to interrupt, Ms. Cavendish, but you have a phone call from Houston. Are you available?"

There could only be one person who'd call her from Houston. Camden Marquess, Special Agent in Charge, Mr. FBI himself. Camden Marquess, who resembled a fine amalgam of Gregory Peck and Sam Elliot.

Available for Camden? Hell, she could've been gasping her last breath and she'd be available for Camden.

Moira sat up and righted her skirt and blouse on the way to her desk, and told Stephanie to have the call put through. She picked it up with the first ring.

"Why, Special Agent in Charge Marquess, how may I help you?"

Moira expected to hear a deep Texas drawl reply, "Do you need to ask, darlin'?"

"Excuse me," a prim female voice said instead. "Am I speaking to Ms. Moira Cavendish?"

Surprised by the no-nonsense feminine voice, Moira checked her phone's display. Yes, the same number. His secretary, perhaps?

"Yes, this is Moira Cavendish. How may I help you?"

"Ms. Cavendish, my name is Hope Langley. I am Agent Marquess's executive secretary. He has listed you as a personal contact should...."

The formality of the woman's voice made Moira catch her breath. The tone of voice suggested bad news would follow. The sudden punch of fear twisted her stomach and made her knees go weak, and Moira fell awkwardly into her leather executive chair.

"Should what, Ms. Langley?"

Moira worked to keep her voice modulated, but she actually wanted to scream, "Say it. Spit it out. He's dead, isn't he?"

"Agent Marquess has been wounded in the line of duty. He is presently in critical condition, and the doctors are saying the next day or two will determine the...." Hope Langley paused for a long moment. "Agent Marquess listed your name in lieu of next of kin. He has no surviving family members to notify."

Moira's brain whirled. Critical condition meant still breathing in her book. She'd unconsciously hunched her shoulders and pulled the phone into the cradle between neck and shoulder but straightened her posture before asking, "What hospital is Agent Marquess in?"

She marveled how, even numb with shock, she could write so legibly, as she jotted the address and ICU room number on her desk calendar.

"Thank you, Ms. Langley. I appreciate the call."

Once off the line, Moira headed right to the cabinet containing her decanter of scotch, poured herself a stiff belt, and knocked it back. She poured another and sipped it while she paced, the better to arrange her thoughts to stop them from darting around her office like rabid squirrels.

One of her revolutions brought her past the fainting couch, and the sight of it forced an unexpected hiccup of a sob from her throat, but she squelched the urge to lose control of her emotions. Even if Cam had been the only one she ever let play on it with her, she wouldn't cry. Dommes didn't cry, but they could shed a few tears in the privacy of their office.

Two more revolutions around her office had her punching her intercom for Stephanie.

When her trusted assistant stuck her head in her office, Moira ordered, "Cancel all of my appointments for the week. I'm going to Houston. I'll return as soon as I can."

Camden Marquess would not be permitted to expire without his Mistress's permission. He would obey her direction and live, or she'd follow him to hell to mete out his punishment.

Chapter Eleven

Orion showed Major Williams the diagram of the course he'd laid out for his students. He wanted to go over it one more time. The course had several moving parts: dogs, search teams, rough terrain. Even the weather had been factored in. High humidity, followed by rain, followed by a slight lessening of the humidity, which was excellent, or they'd have to call the exercise due to heat index warnings. If his students successfully evaded capture before the scheduled ending of the exercise, they would be able to claim justifiable bragging rights.

Orion, as their instructor, thought they were more than up to the challenge. As their instructor, he would not be part of the testing, but he'd come to work early because he couldn't refrain from some last-minute tweaking to ensure his students did well.

Sergeant Russell slammed into the office, white-faced and out of breath. "Oh, thank God you're in early, Gunny."

Orion extended the cup of coffee he'd been about

to drink to the sergeant. He obviously needed it more. "What's up, Sergeant?"

"I got a call from my brother-in-law, Sam Wilson. He and my sister live in a trailer park across the river from Hospital Point. It's not the nicest of places, but it's all they can afford until my brother-in-law makes sergeant." Sergeant Russell took a gulp of coffee and continued. "He called me at four thirty this morning. He gets up to run then, and he went in to check on my niece, only to find her bed empty. He found the screen to her bedroom window lying on the ground outside.

"The trailer they live in is a piece of crap, and the air conditioner went out earlier this week, so they've been sleeping with the windows open. Someone took my niece, Gunny."

Major Lewis left his desk and pulled out a chair for the distraught sergeant. "Okay, Sergeant, has your brother-in-law called the police?"

"Yes, yes he has, sir, but there isn't much they can do until it gets light out." Sergeant Russell turned to face Orion and blurted, "Gunny, if there are any tracks to be found, you can do it. I told my brother-in-law to insist you be part of the effort to find my niece. She's only four, Gunny. She's the sweetest, most trusting little thing. If she knew whoever came to her window, she wouldn't make a fuss."

Orion's stomach soured at the thought of someone taking the child with the intention of harming her in some way. He knew the area around her window had to be preserved for any tracks, and Sergeant Russell's brother-in-law needed to be warned not to trample over any signs that might have been left by the kidnapper.

"Okay, Sergeant, I'll head out there. Call your brother-in-law, tell him I'm on my way, and have him give my name to whatever police show up. Also, tell him to keep everyone away from the window, I don't want them mucking up the trail if there is one."

Orion glanced Major Lewis's way and realized he needed the officer's permission to leave his assigned duty, but before he could speak, the major placed a small form on his desk.

"What's this, sir?"

"It's the sick leave form you forgot to fill out last night. As I recall, you have an appointment at the VA today. Here, I've signed off on it."

"Thanks, Major, but what about my classes? I obviously haven't arranged for anyone to cover them."

"I'll cover them. Have you forgotten we do lesson plans and lecture notes ahead of time? Go, Orion. Find the girl."

Sergeant Russell started to follow Orion, but Major Lewis called him back. "Sergeant Russell, as much as I know you want to be there, you can't miss the material being taught today. It's the last class before the big tracking test, and it has important information in it. The gunny will do his best for you."

Sergeant Russell hung his head and murmured, "Aye, sir," but gave Orion a wordless plea before he left the office.

Orion followed Sergeant Russell's directions to the trailer park. He didn't have to search too hard to find the right trailer; the police cruisers parked in front made it easy.

One of the policemen stationed outside tried to turn him away, but when he stated his name, the father broke away from the cop he was talking to and immediately motioned for Orion to follow him around to the rear of the trailer.

Dismayed to find far too many people there, Orion didn't say anything. He didn't want to be kicked off the search by mouthing off about cops mucking up the trail.

"My brother-in-law says you're the best tracker, Gunny. I'll do whatever I need to do to help you out, so please, God, find something we can follow so I can find the son of a bitch who took my daughter."

"I need to see the area around the window. Can you clear me a little space without someone walking through it?"

"You got it, Gunny."

Sam Wilson went to the cop in charge and pointed at Orion then at the window and the ground.

Orion stood quietly while the cop gave him a long stare then cleared him to enter. He first took note of the footwear everyone had on. He relaxed a little after discovering only two styles of footwear: police-issued shoes and Marine boots, his own included. He started to think better of the police when he realized the area directly under the window had been kept clear of foot traffic.

Another positive factor was the ground under the little girl's window was dirt, not sand. He found a distinct tread mark with the wavy pattern of some kind of sports shoe, probably a sneaker.

Orion followed the trail right down to the water's edge. The sneaker print stopped on the wet bank of the New River. Tracking dogs would be useless unless he could pick up the trail again on dry land.

He needed a boat. A slow-moving bass boat with

a trolling motor would be ideal to hug the water line and help him spot where the man beached his boat.

Okay, time to liaise with the policeman in charge, Sergeant Jablonski. Orion introduced himself and thanked him for letting him have access to the area.

"Gunny Brown, is it? What did you find?"

Orion pointed to the New River. "Well, the man came and left by boat. You can see where he dragged it up on the bank. I'd say, judging by the length of the stride and the depth of the impressions left, you need to search for a short-legged, heavy-set man. He's wearing some sort of sports shoe or sneaker, and he pronates. The right edge of the sneaker is worn down more than the rest of the sole."

Sergeant Jabolonski crammed his spiral notebook back into his suit pocket. "Shit, tracking dogs can't track on water. I can see you're good at what you do, Gunny, but I doubt even you can track through water."

"You're right, Sergeant, but if we use slow-moving boats and trawl along the bank, I might be able to see where he returned to dry land. I don't think whoever took the girl went far. He wouldn't want to be out on the water and chance being spotted by an early shrimp boat or fisherman."

Jablonski pressed his lips together for a five count before replying. "Okay, let me make a few phone calls and set it up. The sooner we find the bastard, the better for the little girl."

The police sergeant got everything organized with a minimum of fuss, and Orion found himself climbing into a boat in record time. The father's vehement insistence he be the one working the boat's engine caused a small delay until Orion waved him in and admonished him to keep quiet and let him concentrate on finding the trail. He gave a nod to Sergeant Jablonski, who followed behind in another boat with three other armed cops.

Lance Corporal Wilson obeyed Orion's directions to the letter, or almost. Orion realized the low white noise he'd been tuning out for the last fifteen minutes came from the father. When he turned to Wilson in inquiry, Orion recognized it as a prayer repeated over and over.

Orion said his own prayer to the Great Spirit. The Great Spirit chose to favor him, and he spotted the fresh divot and the flattened grass and directed Wilson to beach their boat away from the area he wanted to study. He waved for Sergeant Jablonski to do the same.

As soon as Orion oriented himself, he knew the most likely spot they'd find the girl. He'd spent free weekends walking over most of the terrain for miles in either direction because spending a weekend trekking through the woods around Camp Lejeune and Sneads Ferry had been the only way he knew how to relax before he met Dai.

Orion walked slowly forward but stopped occasionally to move away a blade of grass or a twig. The signs told him what he needed to know, and he motioned for Sergeant Jablonski to approach.

Orion went into instructor mode. "You can see the man's prints moving in this direction, and now, over here, you can see them going in the other direction. The ones going forward are heavier or deeper impressions than the ones returning. I believe your kidnapper carried the child going forward, but he didn't have her when he headed back to the water."

Orion kept his voice low while explaining his discovery to the police sergeant, but the father had obviously been listening, for a groan broke the silence. Orion turned and offered him what hope he could.

"I know of a cabin, well, it's more of a rundown shack, directly ahead in a copse of trees. I think your daughter may be there."

Lance Corporal Wilson nodded his head, and Orion breathed a little easier to see a small amount of hope evident on his face. He found none on Sergeant Jablonski's. The cop had too much experience with what happened to four-year-old kids kidnapped in the middle of the night.

Jablonski jabbed a finger, first at Orion then at Lance Corporal Wilson. "Okay, Gunny, lead on, but when we get close to the shack, I want you and the father to stop and let me and my men go forward. You say the man left, but we don't know if he had any accomplices or maybe used a different route."

Jablonski's reasoning made perfect sense to Orion, and he moved out. It didn't take long to get to the dilapidated shack, and Orion motioned for everyone to stop. Upon first sight of the cabin, Sam Wilson surged forward, and Jablonski moved fast to restrain him.

"Easy there, Wilson. You aren't armed, and we don't know who or what might be in that cabin. Let us take it from here."

While Jablonski got the father under control, Orion moved close enough to the side of the cabin to note two trails. The flattened grass showed one leading to the front door, but it also showed one coming from the rear of the cabin.

It caught his attention because there was no obvious reason for using a different exit. The hairs on the back of his neck started to prickle like they used to do on patrol in Afghanistan. Orion's combat spidey sense kicked in, and he ran to the front of the cabin and tackled the cop about to open the front door.

"What the hell are you doing?" The officer huffed as Orion got off him.

"Sorry, but I'm pretty sure the door is booby-trapped. Let's withdraw to a safe distance and I'll show you the signs."

Orion motioned for everyone to move farther away from the cabin, but it became too much for the little girl's father, and Jablonski almost had to tackle him to keep him from rushing inside.

Orion stepped forward and used his Gunnery Sergeant command voice on the Marine.

"Stand down, Marine. I'm pretty sure the door is booby-trapped. If you look at the tracks, the man went in the front and came out the back. There is no good reason for using different paths, unless he rigged something on the front door.

"Since the cabin doesn't have windows, there are only two ways to enter or exit. The logical one would be the front door for anyone trying to find the little girl. Let me check out the rear exit and see what's what."

Jablonski put himself between Orion and the cabin. "Okay, Gunny, but I'm coming with you. You can take the lead because you have more experience with booby-traps, but I'll be covering you."

Jablonski waved for his men to keep an eye on Wilson and stay where they were before following in

Orion's footsteps.

Orion stopped at the rear door and did a slow perusal of the ground around the door, and the small gap where the warped door hadn't closed all the way. There were no pieces of monofilament or any suspicious pile of leaves camouflaging an explosive device.

At Jablonski's nod of permission, he eased the door open and immediately saw he'd been right. The front door *had* been rigged with a shotgun. Whoever opened the front door would've gotten a double blast of deadly pellets.

The sight of the tiny, delicate girl staked like a sacrificial animal to the dirt floor of the shack enraged him. She'd been savagely beaten, and her tiny body had blood in places no four-year-old should be bleeding from.

It crushed his heart when she raised her head enough to see his Marine boot and cammie pant leg and began to cry weakly for her daddy. Jablonski clamped down on his shoulder to prevent him from approaching her.

"Stop right where you are, Gunny. If we want to catch this bastard, we need to have the lowest number of people tramping through here. Just tell me how to keep the shotgun from going off then go outside and wait with the father. My men and I will take it from here. Oh, tell Officer Reader to call for an ambulance. Do you know if there are any roads close by? I don't want to move the girl on foot, but we might have to carry her out if we can't get an ambulance in here."

Orion took out his large pocket knife and gave it to Jablonski. He explained how to disarm the booby-trap then he gave him the bad news.

"There aren't any roads close enough for an ambulance, but there is a clearing on the other side of these trees. It's big enough for a chopper. I'm pretty sure there aren't any phone lines close enough to worry about, so it should be a piece of cake for the chopper to land."

"Okay, then, give Reader the coordinates for the chopper, and, Gunny, whatever it takes, keep this little girl's father from coming in here."

Orion nodded and started to leave but stopped and tugged off his T-shirt. "Here, I think it won't hurt to cover her up. Lance Corporal Wilson shouldn't have to see his daughter naked when they carry her out of here."

Jablonski blew out a long breath before nodding and accepted the T-shirt.

Orion left quickly. He'd have to trust the cop would be gentle with the little girl. He headed back to Wilson, but the sight of his bare chest sent the lance corporal into hysterics.

"She's dead, isn't she? The fucking bastard killed her, didn't he?"

The distraught father tried to run to the cabin, but Orion grabbed him and held on. It took considerable strength to keep the wiry lance corporal contained. He had to put a lock on the man's face, and shout, "Calm down, Lance Corporal," before Wilson stopped trying to break free.

"Rest easy, Wilson. I need to give Officer Reader the coordinates for a chopper to get your little girl to the hospital, and the sooner the better. I'm not going to lie to you, Marine, your daughter is hurt and needs medical attention ASAP. Now, button it up and let these men do their jobs to help your daughter."

The lance corporal's body sagged in relief. Orion had the situation managed. But the lance corporal's daughter cried out in pain, and everything went to hell. *Jablonski probably just freed her from the restraints or tried to cover her with my shirt.*

Before he could resist, Wilson grabbed him in a bear hug, and used his shoulder, once again, to prop up a sobbing Marine. As much as he tried, he couldn't calm the distraught father, until Wilson suddenly went silent. Lance Corporal Wilson had hyperventilated and passed out, taking both of them down to the ground.

Orion sat with the unconscious Marine in his lap, and he held him there as things started happening around them. No one even noticed the two of them sitting in the grass, probably because Gunnery Sergeant Orion Brown had left Onslow County and returned to Helmand Province, Afghanistan, to hold another of his fallen Marines.

It could have been an hour, a second, or a day before a paramedic relieved Orion of his burden to fly Lance Corporal Wilson out in the same chopper as his daughter.

With no clear idea how he'd gotten there, Orion found himself across the river, promising a detective, whose name he didn't catch, to make himself available for further questioning then he drove himself home.

He finally became aware enough to recognize his own living room, and Orion knew he could add another side-effect to his list of unwanted PTSD symptoms, fugue state. The TV he must've switched on at some point named the day as Saturday, but he couldn't recall where the rest of Friday went. He was still in the same dirty cammies but shirtless.

Orion dropped to the floor of his living room and started to cry. Not big wracking sobs like Lance Corporal Wilson's, but a low, keening wail he couldn't stop. The repeated bounce of the dragon dog tag against his chest as he rocked himself made him realize he needed to call his sensei, but what was the point of returning to Dai? Utterly despondent over the setback, Orion's sobs intensified.

Chapter Twelve

D ai stepped out the shower to get ready for this evening's play with Orion. The phone in his bedroom rang, and he ran from the bathroom to grab it before they could hang up. He noted the number displayed on the screen. Orion had never called before.

"Hello?"

No one answered.

"Orion, is that you? Are you there?" Concern swamped him. "Orion?"

"Sensei, I don't think I can be there this evening. Something has happened, and I don't think I can drive."

Immediately concerned, Dai asked, "Did you have an accident?"

"No, Sensei."

The hoarseness in Orion's voice worried Dai. Had his sub been crying? "Orion, tell me what happened? Are you ill?"

His question earned him only a huffed breath in response.

"Tell me what is wrong, Orion," Dai ordered in is best Dom voice. "I want to help, but I need to know what is wrong."

A full minute passed, and while he waited for his answer, he started dressing with one hand so he didn't break the connection.

"No, Sensei, I'm not ill...at least not physically ill. Something happened yesterday, and I can't seem to stop crying. My vision isn't clear enough to drive."

"Orion," Dai shouted over Orion's sobbing. "You will have your door unlocked and be waiting for me in the submissive position. I am leaving my place now. Whatever the problem is, you don't have to face it by yourself. Do you understand me?"

Dai held his breath.

"Yes, Sensei," Orion croaked.

Dai ended the call, threw the phone in the general direction of its charging station, and finished pulling a pair of jeans and a T-shirt over his wet body. He grabbed his helmet and the keys to his bike then flew down the stairs.

With his senses on high alert for cops, Dai cursed the people who tried to cruise in the left lane as he passed them on the right. He couldn't afford to be delayed by getting stopped for speeding.

Orion told him it normally took fifteen minutes to get from the dojo to his house, but Dai made it in ten. Dai pulled his bike next to Orion's truck and parked. He removed his helmet as he ran up the steps and opened the door without knocking. He discovered Orion kneeling on the floor of his living room in the submissive position. He was chagrinned to see Orion had interpreted his command literally. Water still dripped from his sub's body from a recent shower, and he hadn't a stitch on.

Dai knelt down and gently lifted Orion's face. "Oh, Orion, what's the matter, baby?" The exclamation left his mouth before he could censor it. "What has happened? Tell me."

Orion launched himself into his arms, and he had to fight to keep them both upright as Orion clung to him and sobbed. Dai made soothing noises as he edged them toward the sofa.

He'd maneuvered the unresisting man into a sitting position, with most of him in his lap and his head on his shoulder before Orion answered his question.

"I'm sorry, Sensei. I can't seem to stop crying. It started after I got home yesterday and I...I.... Oh God, I can't close my eyes or I'll see them all over again."

"See who, Orion. Tell me, baby, talk to me." Dai combed his fingers through Orion's hair in a soothing motion.

"My men, I'll see the men who cried on my shoulder. I couldn't give them what they wanted."

"What did they want, Orion? Tell me what they wanted."

"They wanted me to fix it. They wanted me to say nothing bad had happened, but I couldn't. I couldn't make them live again. I couldn't fix it. I had to be strong for them, so I couldn't cry, and now I can't stop." Orion wailed the last.

Whoa, something had triggered this response, and if he stood a snowball's chance in Hell of calming Orion down, he needed to know what had happened.

Dai gripped Orion's face and bade him focus on him. "Orion, tell me what happened yesterday."

His sub tried to break eye contact, but Dai

tightened his grip, and forced Orion's gaze to center on him once again. "I will help you any way I can, but I need you to tell me what happened, Orion."

The resistance left Orion's body. Dai gathered the man deeper into his arms and listened to his disjointed accounting.

"Friday morning, Sergeant Russell came to my office and told me his niece had been kidnapped. He wanted me to help the Onslow County Police Department as a tracker. His brother-in-law had called him as soon as he discovered the screen on the window to his daughter's bedroom was off and his daughter missing. He'd gone in to check on her before his run."

Orion drew a shuddering breath. "How could I say no to such a request? Whoever kidnapped the child did leave some signs. Enough signs for me to track them. The trail led right to the New River. The trailer park the Marine lives in abuts the river. Dogs would have been useless.

"I had the police troll along the shoreline until I found the place where the kidnapper beached his boat then I followed the tracks to an abandoned shack.

"I knew the kidnapper had come and gone because I spotted two sets of tracks. One going forward had deeper foot impressions like he was carrying something but not the ones returning. The signs told me whoever kidnapped the girl had not carried her away from the shack, and I pointed those details out to the detective in charge.

"I didn't know if the child still lived, or even if she had been left in the shack, but I didn't want to air my opinion within hearing distance of her father, who'd insisted on being part of the search party. The police had tried to make him stay home, but he'd raised holy hell and gotten to come along.

"Whatever monster took such a sweet little girl hadn't tried to camouflage his moves. The heavier tracks blazed a trail right up to the shack. Luckily, I stopped the cop who volunteered to check it out."

Dai gave Orion a gentle hug. "Why did you stop the cop?" His knees went weak when Orion unconsciously returned the hug.

"Whoever went in didn't come out the same way. His foot impressions were lighter coming out than going in. To me, with my combat experience, it screamed booby-trap, and I told them so, after I tackled the cop who reached for the door. Good thing for him I did. The front door did prove to be booby-trapped. Whoever opened the door would've taken a double-barreled shotgun blast to the chest."

Dai didn't want to, but he had to ask. "And the little girl?"

Orion snuggled in cheek to cheek with Dai. "Alive but badly hurt," he whispered. "The bastard beat her and raped her and staked her out like an animal on the dirt floor."

Dai tried to offer something positive. "I'm proud of you, Orion. You found the girl, and you saved the life of the cop who might've died if he'd opened the door, and—"

Orion cut him off with a sharp swipe of his hand as he left the sofa to pace in front of him. He would have none of Dai's praise.

"When the father learned his daughter still lived but needed immediate medical attention, he collapsed in my arms. I held him while he cried, but he hyperventilated and went limp. It took us both to the ground, and I immediately flashed back to the last Marine I lost in Afghanistan. The one who died in my arms as I held him.

"I managed to hold myself together enough to answer questions from the police investigators, but after I got home, I started crying, and I can't seem to stop. My head is spinning with images, Sensei, and, and...." Orion rubbed his arms and shivered. "And I don't think I'm coming back from this. I lost most of yesterday. I don't even know if I slept or ate in the last twenty-four hours. I've lost my mind, Sensei, and I don't think I want to continue looking for it."

Dai had none of Moira's psychological training, but he could speak from his heart. He stood and placed his hands on Orion's shoulders, the better to see his reaction. "The little girl's father did you a favor, Orion. You couldn't cry for your Marines in Afghanistan because you had to remain strong for their buddies who had to return to combat. But holding the child's father as he cried cracked the wall of reserve you constructed to protect yourself from all the hurt you'd stored inside. It gave you, at last, the chance of honoring your lost Marines by draining the well of tears you've kept inside for so long."

Dai released his grip and led Orion back to the sofa. "You aren't crazy. What you are is crazy strong when you need to be. Cry all you want, Gunny. You found the girl and saved her before she could die of her injuries."

Dai lowered his voice and crooned into Orion's ear. "The father chose your shoulder to cry on because he sensed your strength. He needed comfort, and you gave it. You are unselfishly giving, Orion

Brown, and I am honored to hold you in your grief over the loss of your men. I'm not going anywhere. I'll hold you for as long as you need me to."

As he spoke, he placed small kisses on Orion's temple and his cheek to soothe his distraught sub, but Orion suddenly turned his head and his kiss landed right on Orion's lips, and Dai found his own lips captured by Orion's in a deep, passionate kiss. A kiss he didn't want to end.

Dai's compassion changed to deep lust in a nanosecond, and it took considerable will to continue to soothe and have Orion remain calm enough to respond to his direction. Orion needed to be reminded of his submissive role.

Dai broke the kiss and put a small amount of space between them until Orion took a deep breath and really saw him. Dai slowly bent his head, demanded entry to Orion's mouth, and lost himself in the kiss until Orion began tugging his T-shirt off. Again, he sought space. He needed to see Orion's face to deliver his caution.

"Orion, this is your grief speaking. You know I want you, but I will take you only if you are fully cognizant of what you are doing. I don't want you to be able to say I took advantage of you when you were vulnerable."

"I understand, Sensei, but every fiber of my body is crying out to lose myself in you. If you want me to stand on my deck and proclaim to anyone within listening distance that I want to surrender to you completely, I will."

Dai jerked back at Orion's instant response.

"I want to be taken by the dragon. I need the dragon to devour me. I want it all, Sensei, and I'm communicating this to you in the most open way I can. I want you. I want to feel you inside me. I want to feel skin on skin, not plastic or hard rubber toys. Do you need me to phrase it any other way? I want to feel your body making love to mine."

Dai did the only thing he could in the situation. He rose from the sofa and kicked off his shoes before he stripped off his shirt and jeans.

"Come, Orion, show me to your bedroom."

Orion didn't resist as he led him to the bed and remained pliant as he used lube to anoint the opening.

"I'm going to go slowly. I don't want to hurt you, Orion. If you change your mind, use your safe word."

For the first time in a long while, Dai didn't know what to expect. He'd never made love to a man. He had no idea what would give pleasure or pain for his sub. He needed verbal guidance from Orion.

"Orion, talk to me. I want to know what pleases you, and I especially want to know if you feel uncomfortable with what I'm doing."

His sub readily complied soon after he began, and Dai listened, not only to the words, but also the silent communication given by Orion's body.

"Ah, keep using a shallow stroke, the initial discomfort is passing. Yesss, don't stop."

Dai dared to go deeper after a few minutes, and when Orion did not shy away from the penetration, deeper still. At last, completely seated, he stopped.

"No, don't stop, Sensei. You aren't hurting me."

Having been given permission, Dai withdrew almost all the way before slamming himself home. Orion's grunt of pleasure thrilled him. He strove to return the pleasure until the imminence of his own orgasm fixed his concentration on himself. Even so, he shared. Dai heightened Orion's sensation by stroking his penis with long, firm strokes.

"Come with me, Orion. I want us to come together. Say it, say you're mine."

"Yesssss, Sensei. Yours, I'm yours, oh God, I'm close, very close. Ahhh, Kenji! Oh my God, Kenjiiii!"

With the first utterance of his given name, Dai exploded. He collapsed atop Orion and sent them both sprawling facedown on the mattress.

Dai woke to the sensation of Orion's fingertips caressing his eyebrows. Angling his body into Orion's, he kissed him and snuggled in closer. "Will you hold me, Kenji? I want to fall asleep in your arms. I think I'll be able to sleep if you're holding me."

After caring for Orion and cleaning himself, Dai either fell asleep or passed out with Orion's head on his shoulder and his leg thrown over his thighs. His entire body hummed with the close physical contact. His surfeit of sexual satisfaction precluded delving deeper into the psychology of what had just occurred. He only knew the fire he'd carried in his belly since he first touched Orion had been banked, and the embers warmed and comforted him.

Chapter Thirteen

O rion awoke languidly. He never even thought of getting out of bed as he glanced to the side, searching for Kenji. Finding only empty space, he had a moment of panic he'd dreamed the whole love scene. Not until he scanned to the end of his king-size bed did he find Kenji sitting, totally nude, in the lotus position, with his eyes closed.

Kenji's lips moved, but he made no sound. Could he be praying? Orion didn't want to interrupt, so he simply settled into the pillows and watched the morning sun move splashes of light over Kenji's deeply sculpted body. Orion found himself growing hard as he feasted his eyes on Kenji.

He must have made some small sound, for Kenji suddenly turned his way, and those beautiful jade orbs made Orion's desire soar. The man didn't know how his beauty affected him, so he kept it to himself while he studied how Kenji's hair fell right above his shoulders, and how the sunlight sent blue sparks through it. The dragon on his right pectoral grinned a good morning to him.

He didn't move as Kenji rose in one fluid movement and approached the side of the bed.

"Good morning, Orion. You were sleeping so peacefully, I didn't want to wake you. Is there anything I can get for you?"

"You shaved your pubic hair." He'd meant to ask in return what, if anything, he could do for his Dom, but what came out shocked him.

Kenji grinned for a fleeting moment, and Orion squeezed his eyes closed in abject embarrassment.

"Ah, yes, I did."

Orion opened his eyes at his sensei's voice.

"You did say you wanted me to. Have your changed your mind? If you don't like it, the hair will grow again."

Orion grabbed Kenji's waist and pulled him closer to the side of the bed. The man's wide eyes told him he'd surprised him. "No, I like it very much. It will make doing what I've wanted to do since my last punishment much more pleasurable."

Kenji went still as a stone in his embrace. "And what is it you want to do, Orion?"

"I'm thirsty, Kenji, but it isn't coffee I want this morning."

Orion sat up and took Dai into his mouth, until he grew long and firm. Dai's small mewl of pleasure urged him to continue. Kenji's exotic flavor made his tongue tingle, and Orion happily tried to tie a knot in his dick with his tongue, as he would a cherry stem. He knew it was impossible, but, by the way Kenji moaned his enjoyment, he'd attained the desired effect. He only stopped when Kenji tugged at his hair.

"Orion, wait, wait a minute. I want to tell you

something."

Orion stopped laving Kenji with his tongue, but continued to place wet kisses up and down his sensei's dick while he waited for an explanation.

"Orion, I want more than this. I'm a greedy Dom. I want it all. Please, Orion, let me have it all. Ride the dragon."

Orion eased away from the edge of the bed and waited for Kenji to crawl in then found the tube of lubricant where it had been tossed on the nightstand. His entire body shook as he slowly covered the scales of the dragon in kisses as he applied the slippery ointment. His heart beat almost too hard to speak as he positioned himself behind Kenji.

"I'm only going to ask this once, or I'll lose my nerve. I need to know your safe word, Kenji."

Orion waited until Kenji turned his head and gave him a shy grin.

"Snowflake. My safe word is snowflake."

Once again, he caressed the length of the dragon's body and watched as it rippled in pleasure. "Are you sure, Kenji?"

"Yes, absolutely. It's what I've wanted since our first session, but these feelings confused me. Last night ended the confusion for me, Orion. I've accepted your surrender, and now I want to give you mine. However, if you've changed your mind, if you don't want to accept what I want to give, please stop now."

Orion skimmed his fingertips down the back of the dragon. "And miss riding the most beautiful dragon I've ever seen? Not a chance in hell."

Orion entered Kenji in one long, slow stroke until securely seated. Kenji immediately pushed back and moved forward again.

Nope, not happening. Kenji would not be allowed to set the pace, for they'd switched roles. Orion grabbed Kenji by the waist and rammed himself home again. The sensation tore an approving hiss from him.

"Yesss! Kenji, I know I should take this slow and gentle, but I don't have the control. I want to fuck you until we both shout our pleasure. You must tell me to stop if I hurt you. Promise me you'll tell me if it becomes too intense."

"I promise, promise, promise, but there's no need to slow down. Sky, I've wanted you so long now, it isn't possible to restrain myself. Yes, faster, I'm close, so close. Ahhh, Sky! Yesss, Sky!"

With the first pump of Kenji's release, Orion came hard enough to temporarily blind him. His body pumped in rhythm with Kenji's until they stopped and toppled to the side, still joined. Now he matched Kenji's panting.

It took him several seconds to get enough air into his lungs to cry, "Oh my God, I think I'm dead." The ridiculousness of his exclamation started them both laughing, and he had to withdraw or die all over again. He gathered Kenji deeper into his arms and put his head under his chin to snuggle.

Orion didn't waste the opportunity but slowly petted the dragon until he went to sleep. It didn't take him long to follow suit.

Orion popped awake when his growling stomach developed an echo. He found Kenji lying with his arm propped on the pillow, watching him.

"I'm glad you are awake. I'm starving. Can we

have breakfast now?"

The innocent question posed a conundrum for Orion. What should he call his Dom? Dare he assume they could continue to be lovers, or would they return to being sensei and sub? Kenji settled the matter.

"C'mon, Sky, I think my stomach is trying to claw its way out of my body. I skipped dinner last night, and so did you. I need meat and bread and coffee. Do you have any breakfast materials?"

"Bacon and egg sandwiches and coffee coming right up, Kenji. Let me hop into the shower. I promise to make it a quick one then you can shower while I fix breakfast."

He started to rise, but Kenji tackled him from behind, and he found himself spread-eagled on the mattress with Dai's lips locked to his. Another rumble from Dai's stomach ended the kiss, and he hit the shower.

Showered and shaved, he sought out Kenji and found him still nude but sitting in his living room, watching the passing shrimp boats. Orion left him to it while he started on breakfast. He did take a moment to appreciate the perfect male body when Kenji rose and stalked toward him.

"May I borrow a pair of briefs or boxers? I didn't take time to put a pair on last night."

"Sure thing. How about I also lend you a pair of shorts? You promised to go kayaking with me this morning, and you'll be too warm in jeans."

Kenji followed him into the bedroom and thanked him for the clothes. Orion also gave him a still-wrapped toothbrush.

***

Dai soon found kayaking to be almost a Zen experience. The quiet on the water and the closeness to nature had a very calming effect, especially to a body still tingling from his lover's caresses.

He'd listened to Orion's instructions, and now paddled like a pro from the front of the two-man kayak, but deferred to his lover's directions in steering them to a particular destination. Sky had even packed them a lunch in a small cooler.

The Zen feeling evaporated quickly after he pointed to a tree overhanging the narrow waterway, and a black rope detached itself from the tree and fell into the kayak.

Whoa, not a rope, Dai realized, as it began slithering from the prow of the kayak straight for him. He waited for the right moment and quickly picked the snake up and flung it from the boat then resumed paddling.

"Oh my God, Kenji, are you all right? The snake didn't bite you, did it? Fuck, I'm sorry. I should have warned you snakes like to hang out on trees over the water. Normally, I would have steered around the tree, but this part of the canal is too narrow to avoid it."

"I'm fine, Sky. No, the snake didn't bite me. Why? Was it poisonous?"

"Yes. Water moccasins are extremely aggressive. Man, I can't believe the way you snatched it up and flung it away before I even had a chance to warn you. The speed of your reflexes is awesome. I wish I had had a chance to capture that on my camera's video app. Your students would be most impressed. Ah, here we are, the place I told you about."

Dai listened to Orion's instructions for how to get out of the kayak and held it steady for Orion to disembark. They pulled the kayak farther up the bank and approached the massive willow tree.

"How good are you at climbing trees?" Orion held aside a curtain of willow branches so he could enter the green living cave created by the overhanging branches.

"It all depends, Sky. Are there more water moccasins to be found in this tree? If there are, I'll pass. I don't want to tempt fate. Truthfully, I've never climbed a tree before. There aren't a lot of trees to be found in dojos."

Dai had to look up when he finished speaking. Orion had climbed the tree very quickly and sat on a wide branch peering down at him like a large wood sprite.

"Come on up, Kenji. If you jump, you can catch the branch and pull yourself up, but first toss the cooler bag up here. We'll eat in the tree."

Dai tossed Sky the bag and pulled himself up to sit next to Orion with his legs hanging down as they ate the sandwiches.

"I've wanted to climb a tree since I saw the willow trees behind Moira's dungeon. I didn't do it there because I didn't want to ruin my suit. But now I'm going to climb to the top and appreciate the view. If you put your feet in the same place as mine, you should make it up there without falling."

Dai heard the challenge and followed his sub up to a vantage spot that did, indeed, offer a beautiful panoramic view of the waterway. He paid attention as

Orion pointed out interesting spots.

He became almost dizzy as the spirit of *wuchang* washed over him. It told him this particular moment had deposited memories and would soon leave, never to be experienced again. He slowed his thoughts down to savor it, but it made him a touch sad. He had taken a lover and experienced him for the first time. He wouldn't be able to do this ever again with Orion. There would never again be a first time for them.

He knew Orion saw everything, so he didn't flinch when his arm encircled his waist.

"What? What has made the beautiful dragon sad?"

How could he explain *wuchang* to his sub, his lover? Dai tried, and Orion listened carefully.

"No, Kenji, there won't be another first time," Orion whispered in his ear. "But there will be a second and a third and a fourth, until we lose count or agree to part, and, unless I'm mistaken, neither one of us is thinking of parting anytime soon."

Dai's reflective mood disappeared, and he leaned in.

"No, Sky." He kissed Orion's lips. "Not anytime soon."

Chapter Fourteen

Moira nodded at the pair of women who entered the hospital elevator with her and said a silent prayer of thanks people didn't try and befriend people in hospital elevators. Her flight to Houston had been uneventful, but the closer she got to the hospital the more unsettled she became. She couldn't believe this might be the last time she held Cam Marquess or got excited by an adorable Texas drawl.

Of all her clients, Cam held a special place in her heart. Oh, Dai Waleska and Orion Brown were two others she could think of, but Camden held first place by being an alpha's alpha who preferred, no, needed to be a submissive. Cam ruled in the world of men, but she ruled his private world.

She served as his petcock, letting out the pressure his high-powered job built up. When Cam submitted to her control, he didn't need to be in charge, and he didn't want to be. In fact, he often bemoaned the fact he could only avail himself of her services twice a year on his annual vacations.

The elevator came to a stop, and Moira returned to the here and now. Not her floor. She stood aside and let the other occupants out. One more floor to go, and her stomach tightened in apprehension. How would she find Camden? Would he be awake? Would he be in pain? Sooner than she liked, the elevator doors opened on the correct floor, and Moira found herself in the ICU. The hushed atmosphere felt like a predatory one. Would the residents live or die?

Moira shook her head to rid it of such morbid thoughts and began counting the room numbers. Each room she passed exposed a new bit of misery, and her stomach roiled. Too many machines attached to too-still patients, too-gray skin colors, too many somber-faced people sitting by the beds. Camden didn't belong here.

Ah, Room 214. Moira stopped at the room's sliding door. The room lacked a patient, but did have rumpled sheets like Cam had been in there but whisked away. Her vision blinked in and out over Cam's possible destination, and she clutched the side of the door for support.

"Excuse me. May I help you?"

Moira whirled around and confronted one of the ICU nurses. "Yes, yes you can. I've come to see Camden Marquess. Where is he? He isn't—"

"Oh, Mr. Marquess had surgery this morning. He's presently in recovery, and they'll be bringing him up, shortly. I don't think it will be long now, if you care to wait."

Moira could only wonder if all ICU nurses took courses on how to remain cheerful while delivering grave news. She drew in a deep breath. "Surgery? I thought he'd already had surgery for the gunshot wound. What happened? Did he have complications?"

The nurse, who couldn't have been more than in her early twenties, tilted her head. "Are you a relative of Mr. Marquess?"

Moira wanted to grab her by her cutesy scrubs and shake her but forced a smile instead and used her silky Mistress voice. "Yes, I'm his next of kin."

Next of kin was a less important relationship than Dominatrix in her book, but if it gave her the right to know Cam's status, she'd give them what they wanted to hear.

"Oh, Mr. Marquess received two wounds. The gunshot wound, which we treated immediately, and an eye injury. Our eye surgeon couldn't fit him in until this morning."

"And what is Agent Marquess's status? Is he still listed in critical condition?" Once again, Moira wanted to shake the information out of the nurse as she dimpled prettily.

"You'll have to ask his attending physicians," she replied, evading her question. "They should be making rounds in the next hour or two. Can I get you anything? A cup of coffee or a bottle of water?"

Moira capitulated to the power-to-be, for the moment. "Yes, a cup of coffee would be most welcome, thank you."

Moira grimaced with the first sip of the battery acid the ICU served its visitors and searched for a place to get rid of it. She stopped and discreetly put the cup on the nightstand. A smartly dressed woman walked into Cam's room, and the woman mirrored her own initial reaction as she gaped at the rumpled sheets and took a step back from the empty bed.

"He's in recovery. They've just operated on his eye injury," she informed the visitor.

Rather than being thankful for the information, the woman spun around and gave her attitude. "And you are?"

Moira grinned, although she wanted to snatch the woman bald, but her roots were in the South, and she knew how to don the Southern belle, butter-won't-melt-in-my-mouth persona. "My name is Moira Cavendish. I am listed as Agent Marquess's next of kin. Whom do I have the pleasure of addressing?"

Her name must have carried some *cachet* she wasn't aware of, for the woman visibly softened after she said her name.

"Oh, Ms. Cavendish, I am so glad you came. I know Agent Marquess will be glad to see you. I'm Hope Langley. This is the first opportunity I've had today to break away and check on him. I try to come each day, but with Agent Marquess out of the office, it's been difficult."

Softening toward Cam's executive assistant for her genuine concern for her boss, Moira gave her what little she knew and asked a few questions of her own.

"The nurse told me he needed surgery for his eye injury, and they performed it this morning. He's in recovery now, and they'll be bringing him up, shortly. Have you been kept abreast of his status? Is he expected to make a full recovery?"

The sliding glass door to Cam's room whooshed open, and Moira broke off her interrogation of Hope Langley to watch an orderly wheel Cam into the room. The ICU nurse followed, and they had him off the gurney and snugged in his bed before Moira could catch her breath.

Although she wanted to ask a million questions, she held her tongue while they reconnected the tubes to her sub's body, straightened sheets, and pushed buttons. Only when the various machines attached to Cam beeped within normal registers did they withdraw.

Moira chanced a glance at Hope Langley and realized she really cared for Cam, but judging by the two carat ring on the marriage finger, not in a romantic way. Hope confirmed it when she turned to face her.

"I hate seeing him this way. Agent Marquess is the most vibrant man I've ever met. He is a superman, and to see him laid low is...awful. I'm not sure I did right by calling you, but he had no other close family to contact, and he spoke so highly of you. He always returned from vacation a much more relaxed person. I know he visited you because I arranged his travel itinerary.

"I won't intrude on your visit. I'm going to go home to cook dinner for my family, and have a glass or three of wine. If you need anything, anything at all, call me, and I will arrange it." Hope Langley gave Moira her business card and left.

Moira approached Cam's bedside and bit her lip to keep the sob inside. Whatever anesthesia they'd given him for his surgery hadn't completely left his body, and it made him seem pale and shrunken as he slept. The bandage covering his left eye added to the effect of frailty.

Moira knew Cam's broad shoulders, chiseled features, and thick chestnut hair increased any red-blooded female's pulse, if they were lucky enough to spot him, but today he appeared shrunken and unable to best his weight in feathers. White-hot anger at whoever had done this to her sub zinged through Moira. She would fix this, starting now, and leaned over to whisper in Cam's ear.

He remembered the anesthesiologist saying something about going night-night right before he took the express train to Nod. He floated in the land of blissful sleep until a beautiful scent filled his nostrils. Huh, who knew anesthesia smelled like perfume? He tried to pin the scent down, but it eluded him. The name didn't matter; he liked it.

Cam turned his head, the better to smell where it came from. Now he could hear a voice, perhaps a radio. He had a hard time distinguishing words, and he strained to hear.

Uh-oh, the voice, so honeyed and soft, had turned strident. What had he done? Had he screwed up an assignment? While he didn't think so, he couldn't concentrate enough to puzzle it out. The drugs made him fuzzy. Yeah, drugs, he was drugged to the gills, but why? Cam frowned in his semi consciousness.

Something pressed his cheek, and the perfume scent grew stronger. The contact warmed him, and, wanting more, he leaned into it. The name of the scent still escaped him, and the puzzle of it hurt his head. He groaned in frustration.

Okay, if he concentrated hard, he could flutter his eyelids. Damn, someone must have glued them shut because it shouldn't be this difficult to open them. Only one of them obeyed his open sesame command, and his fuddled brain began a childish refrain: Stick, struck, stuck, stick, struck, *bang*. Bang? Even with an addled brain he knew bang didn't rhyme with stuck or struck. His brain took a giant leap in logic. So okay, not a rhyme, an occurrence. Cam gave a full-body jerk when he made the connection. He heard a gun go bang, he struck the floor, and now his eye appeared to be stuck. Next up in the brainteaser category was finding out whose gun it was. Bang, bang, bank, ah, bank, as in a place where people put money.

And thank you, Jesus, the random word association solved the puzzle. He remembered. He and Agent Southwick had gone to the bank to question the manager one more time. Things didn't add up, correction, they did add up, but not in a legitimate way. Money laundering constituted a federal offense, and the FBI's forensic accountant had discovered the bank manager had used creative math to help a foreign nation not on the friend of the United States list.

The manager must have expected to get caught because, as soon as he flashed his credentials, the man opened his desk drawer, pulled out a gun, and didn't even hesitate. He hit the floor with a bullet in his chest before he could even say, "Damn, buckaroo, that smarts."

At least the agent who'd accompanied him had enough presence of mind to pull out his own government-issue weapon, and make a deposit the manager wouldn't be refunding in this lifetime.

He got served an extra helping of bad luck because the crook pulled the trigger on his way to hell, and the bullet went into the marble floor and sent a sliver of the marble into his eye. He lost interest in what happened after that.

With memory came situational awareness, and Cam opened his one working eye in a familiar but blurry hospital room to the accompaniment of a voice whispering threats of dire punishment in his ear. Once he could actually make sense of the words, the elusive scent identified itself. Coco Chanel. Only one woman he knew wore Coco Chanel. Moira. Moira had come to his bedside.

He croaked out a greeting. "Hello, darlin'."

"Excuse me? I don't believe you were taught to greet your Mistress in such a way."

"No, Mistress. Forgive me?"

"You are forgiven for now, but it doesn't mean you won't be punished after you've recovered."

Cam curled his lip at his floppy arm when he tried to lift it to touch Moira. *Damn drugs.* He wanted to touch her, but his sad excuse for an arm fell far short of his target. She picked up his hand and placed it on the side of her face, and he treated her to a lopsided grin.

He'd grinned because he hadn't wanted to touch Moira on the face. If he had to be punished for his verbal transgression, it made sense to go all out and cop a feel.

"I dream about your breasts."

Oh. My. God. He knew he'd said it because he heard his voice saying it. What in the hell had they given him for anesthesia, sodium pentothal? It might have been what he'd dreamed about while lying in this hospital bed, but actually saying it made him wish he had enough strength to reach the window so he could jump and end his mortification.

"Sorry, Mistress. I'm pretty high at the moment."

Moira cupped his face and placed a soft kiss on his lips. "You are temporarily forgiven, Special Agent in Charge Marquess. However, I didn't give you permission to get yourself shot, so there will be punishment meted out at your next session with me.

"In case you've forgotten, you are *my* sub, and I will not have you mar your body with punctures from bullets or other sharp objects. I can see some rosy butt cheeks in your future, SAC Marquess.

He had enough residual anesthesia in his system to keep him from becoming aroused at the mention of a spanking from Moira, which was a good thing, and the catheter attached to his pecker agreed with him. *Hmmm, catheter plus a hard-on? Nope, not a good combo.* Somewhere in the pondering of the physical effects of becoming aroused with a tube shoved up his dick, Cam fell sound asleep.

Moira entwined Cam's long fingers with hers and played with the signet ring on his right pinkie finger. She'd given it to him as the visible sign of her Dominance. She'd wondered if he took it off as soon as he returned to Texas. Now she knew the truth. Cam never took it off.

Most people thought the letters stood for Camden Marquess, but, actually, if you studied the ring closely, the capital C stood for Cavendish, Moira Cavendish. Their private joke that they had the same initials, only reversed.

Fairly certain Cam would survive his injuries, Moira began to wonder where the hell his doctor had disappeared to. Maybe this doctor didn't make rounds until after midnight, but just as well. Cam had fallen asleep right after his surprising announcement, and he hadn't awakened. He appeared to be sleeping peacefully. Her sleep the night before hadn't been as restful.

She left Cam's room reluctantly, but she thought it a waste of time to sit by a patient's bedside and watch them sleep. She'd return tomorrow morning, and this time she'd raise enough hell they'd send his physician in to return calm to the ICU.

And return she did, bright and early. She found Cam sitting up and staring in disbelief at the breakfast on his tray table. She didn't even get a chance to say hello before her sub voiced his disapproval of hospital fare.

"Ah, darlin', they're killing me here. They have me on rations a rat wouldn't eat. Can you believe they've given me cold oatmeal, dry toast, weak coffee, and...and prunes? For the love of God, who gives prunes to a man confined to bed? I don't suppose I could talk you into bringing me some *huevos rancheros*?"

Moira laughed at Cam's woebegone expression. "I don't think your surgeon wants you eating spicy food yet. And a good morning to you, Agent Marquess. I will make a rare exception and forgive you twice for not giving me a proper greeting."

"Ah, Mistress, I'm sorry. I woke up this morning wondering if I'd dreamed you, or if you had really come to see me."

Moira wanted to fluff his pillows and certain other parts of Cam's anatomy when he looked away and blushed. "I didn't say anything odd while I was doped up, did I?"

Moira never got the chance to answer the

question because a very young, very handsome Indian doctor walked into the room.

"Good morning, Agent Marquess. You have more color this morning. I'm going to take a little peek at your incision, but first you must introduce me to this lovely visitor."

Cam pushed the uneaten food away and made the introductions. "Dr. Raj Gupta, this is Moira Cavendish. Moira, Doctor Gupta has all of the nurses in love with him, so don't be surprised if he tries to work his magic on you."

"My gracious, Agent Marquess, must you give all my secrets away. Now I'll have to work even harder to put this beauty under my suave Indian charm. At least I have the advantage of being mobile. I like the advantage it gives me when my competition is incapacitated."

"Then you must have been the one who ordered my breakfast this morning. Come on, Doc, they have me on a low-salt diet. I need food a man can eat if you expect me to leave here in good health."

"Hmm, complaining about the hospital food is always a good sign. If you wouldn't mind stepping out of the room, Ms. Cavendish, I'll make my examination quick."

Moira left the room as the doctor drew the curtain across the sliding door. She walked up and down the corridor, until she peeked into one of the rooms and saw a man sound asleep with his mouth open, and attached to far too many tubes—not at all what she wanted to see this early in the morning. She returned to stand outside Cam's room.

The doctor soon had the curtain open again and gestured for her to enter. "Agent Marquess is healing well. He should be well enough to leave here by the end of the week."

"So soon?" Moira couldn't believe someone who'd taken a bullet to the chest would be released so quickly.

"Your friend can count himself very lucky, Ms. Cavendish. The bullet managed to miss anything vital to continued existence. We like to release patients as soon as possible to avoid infection and pneumonia. As hard as hospitals try to keep the germs down, it is impossible to prevent them from occurring."

"What about his vision? Has it been affected?"

"Ah, lovely lady, you'll have to speak with Dr. Solomon. He's the ophthalmologist." Dr. Gupta grinned and turned to Cam. "I'll rescind the no-salt diet, Agent Marquess, but this is a hospital, not a five-star restaurant. Bland is the standard they aspire to here, but if you get hungry enough, you'll find you can eat it."

Moira watched as Cam tilted his head to the side to watch his doctor leave, and wasn't surprised to see a devilish glint come into his unbandaged eye. Her sub was up to something.

"Can a man at least have a kiss if he can't have a decent breakfast?"

Moira played along. "A man can possibly have a kiss if he asks his Mistress in the correct manner."

"Mistress, may I have a kiss?"

"You may."

Moira bent over the bed to offer her lips to Cam.

"Mistress, would you please draw the curtains? I don't want to kiss you in this fishbowl of a room. I want to have you all to myself, or at least have it seem like I do."

"I will humor your request, but only because you have been wounded, Camden Marquess."

Moira pulled the curtain across the door and returned to Cam's bedside. "Now, then, where were we?"

"You were about to bend down so I could kiss you, Mistress."

Moira picked up the bed's remote and lowered the mattress so she didn't have to stretch to kiss Cam. Her wounded sub shocked the hell out of her when she leaned in to kiss him, and he began unbuttoning the suit jacket to her coffee-colored pants suit.

"Camden, what are you doing?"

"I'm trying to kiss you, Mistress."

"But you are unbuttoning, oops, you've unbuttoned my jacket."

"Did I forget to say kiss your breasts, Mistress? I've missed the sight of your sweet, pink aureoles with the light-lavender nipples. Please, Mistress, I need to kiss them. I need to know I'm not dreaming and you're not just a figment of my overactive imagination."

"Oh, Cam, you've the soul of a poet," Moira murmured, as he deftly unclasped the front of her bra and took one of her breasts in his mouth.

"Ah, thank you, my darlin' Mistress. I want to spend hours on each of your breasts, but I am not unmindful of where we are," Cam whispered, as he expertly closed her bra and re-buttoned her jacket.

As Moira straightened and stepped away from the bed, Cam ruefully pointed to the tent he'd erected in the sheet. "And I am also extremely thankful they removed the catheter this morning."

Moira roared with laughter, and, for the first

time in days, she permitted herself to take a deep breath and stop worrying. Her sub could definitely be counted on to stay among the living.

"Pay attention, Agent Marquess. If you want another such kiss, you will have to return to The Willows to get it, but it won't come without a good spanking across my knee."

"Then I'll see you soon, my darlin' Mistress. I am entitled to convalescent leave, and I intend to take all of it."

"Excellent. Your first spanking will be on the antique couch in my office, and I may or may not let you kiss me afterward." She started backing out of the room but stopped at the doorway and gave him a lascivious wink.

The sight of Cam giving her woebegone puppy dog eyes because she'd announced her imminent departure made her want to rush to his side and coddle him until he got his discharge papers. But Moira had a steel backbone and simply blew him a kiss as she left.

Her laughter brightened the ICU corridor when her sub called out, "I abso-fucking love your couch, Mistress."